Maddy swallowed. "I gue... jump in. Please don't inter... want when I'm finished."

"Sounds fair to me," Jordan said stiffly.

Maddy cleared her throat and began. "It says in the Bible that the truth will make me free. And I'm telling you this because I need to be free. . .So I've asked you here tonight so that I can be honest with you. A long time ago, I fell in love with my next-door neighbor. At least, I thought I was in love. But when I met him again, he wasn't the same person. I plotted and schemed about how I could get him to notice me. . . But like I said, he wasn't the same person." Maddy stopped and drank a sip of water, while avoiding eye contact with Jordan.

"When I realized I was falling in love with him, I started praying about it. I was scared to open up and be honest, but one day I was praying, and I remembered the verse that says the truth will make me free. I've been trying to hide it and deny it, but now I know for sure. And even though I don't know how he feels about me, I know I have to say this." Maddy took a deep breath and looked across the table, locking gazes with Jordan. "I love you, Jordan Sanders."

AISHA FORD resides with her parents and younger sister in Missouri. Through her writing, Aisha hopes to present a message of complete trust in Jesus Christ. "The best guide for living is to follow the biblical example of Jesus—the route by which we will reap the most lasting rewards," Aisha says. "Though none of us is perfect, God is the inventor of grace—and He is patient above and beyond what we can ask or imagine."

Books by Aisha Ford

HEARTSONG PRESENTS
HP362—Stacy's Wedding

The Wife Degree

Aisha Ford

Heartsong Presents

A note from the author:
I love to hear from my readers! You may correspond with me by writing:

Aisha Ford
Author Relations
PO Box 719
Uhrichsville, OH 44683

ISBN 1-58660-069-9

THE WIFE DEGREE

Cover illustration by Ron Hall.

PRINTED IN THE U.S.A.

one

Madison Thompson yawned, stretching out on the chaise lounge in her parents' sunroom. As the warm, cozy May sunshine spilled in from all sides, Maddy closed her eyes and considered taking a long, delicious nap. "After all, I deserve it," she said to herself. She'd just completed her last semester at Texas Southern University, and now she was back home in Kansas City for good.

She opened her eyes and sighed comfortably, pushing away the nagging feeling that she should really be unpacking all of the boxes she'd brought home from school yesterday evening.

Her eyelids were growing heavier by the moment, so she reached for one of her mom's comfy couch pillows and snuggled into position for a nap. The boxes could wait. . .the nap couldn't.

"Maddy?" her mother, Berniece, peeked in the room. "Dad and I are going to do a little shopping. We'll be back in a couple hours. Do you need anything?"

Maddy opened her eyes. "As long as you get back in time for dinner, I'll be fine. If you leave it up to me to cook, it'll be something like lunch meat sandwiches or canned soup," she laughed.

Her mom laughed too. "It's your dad who's the slowpoke shopper, but I'll try to get him to speed things up a little by reminding him that we have a hungry daughter waiting for dinner."

"Thanks, Mom. If the house seems really quiet when you get back, don't worry. I'll probably be in here sleeping."

"Thanks for the tip, but you're forgetting that we're used to it being quiet ever since you went away to school. The only time it's ever noisy anymore is when you're home on vacation."

"I guess you're going to have to get used to the noise again because it looks like I'm back for a while," Maddy joked.

"Don't worry about us. We're as happy as can be right about now," Berniece said as she left the room.

Maddy closed her eyes again and listened to the garage door going up, then down. As the sound of her parents' car driving away grew faint, Maddy felt herself drifting to sleep.

Not even five minutes later, she heard a dog whimpering. She groaned and put the pillow over her head to mask the sound.

Much to her disappointment, the whimpering didn't stop but grew even louder. Maddy sat up and looked around. Apparently, the sunroom was too close to the great outdoors for her to get a decent nap. She stood up and decided to go to her room to finish the job she'd started. As she walked past the door that led out to the deck, a movement in the corner of her eye caught her attention. Startled, she turned to get a better look and saw a muddy golden retriever puppy with his paws on the door. When she moved closer, it began wagging its tail at a frenzied pace.

Maddy put her hand on the doorknob, then hesitated. She was not a big fan of pets of any kind, especially muddy ones. And her mother would not be happy if this little ball of energy got loose in her sunroom. Plus, it could be rabid or just plain mean. Maddy tilted her head and looked at the little dog again. He looked harmless, so she decided to slip outside and see if he had any type of identification she could use to return him to his owner.

Cautiously, she opened the door a crack and slid outside, keeping the puppy from getting inside. Then she knelt down and tried to get a look at his collar. "Calm down, you little mud puddle," she said as she reached for his neck. The dog jumped up and down, yipping excitedly.

Maddy sighed. "Well, I can't let you in my parents' house,

and I can't take you home if you don't sit still."

As though he understood what she was saying, the puppy sat still long enough for Maddy to check his collar. Maddy checked once, then twice, but the results were the same. No tags. "A lot of good that did," she said.

She stood up and looked around, hoping to see the puppy's owner nearby. The puppy jumped up and left his muddy signature on her legs. She looked down at him. "Rule number one—keep your paws off my legs," she told him. The puppy sat down, tilted his head sideways, and lifted his floppy ears.

Maddy walked down the deck stairs and around to the front yard with the puppy at her heels. Mrs. Myston, a neighbor who lived across the street, was outside working on her flower beds. Maddy waited to make sure no cars were coming before she crossed the street, knowing her new friend was right behind her.

The puppy bounded across the street ahead of her and headed right to Mrs. Myston's newly planted impatiens. Mrs. Myston chased him away from the flower beds and said, "Oh, no, you don't. I just replanted the ones you dug up last week." She smiled at Maddy and said, "Hello, Madison. Your mother told me you were getting home some time this week. I saw you got in last night."

"I sure did, and I'm glad to be home for good." Maddy smiled. Mrs. Myston saw everything that happened on the block. She acted as though it were her job to know all the goings-on of the neighborhood.

Mrs. Myston returned her attention to the puppy, who was sitting still for the moment. She shook her head and exhaled. "Now why on earth did you bring him over here, Madison?"

Maddy put up her hands to plead her innocence. "I found him on our deck. I was wondering if you knew who he belongs to."

Mrs. Myston pointed across the street to the house next door to Maddy's. "The Sanders. Actually, he belongs to their son. . .you remember Jordan, don't you? The one who had all the girlfriends in high school."

Maddy nodded. *How can I forget him?* she thought. Jordan Sanders had been the only boy she'd ever truly had a crush on. She'd decided in the second grade that he was the most handsome boy she'd ever seen, and from then on, her infatuation had grown. To put it simply, he was tall, dark, and handsome. Years of playing basketball had produced muscles on top of muscles on his six-foot-three frame. His skin was a deeply bronzed shade of mahogany, and he'd always worn his hair so closely shaven that from a distance, he appeared to be bald. His face was almond-shaped, enhanced by a broad nose, full lips, and dark brown eyes. Maddy sighed. She hadn't seen him in at least two years, maybe even three, and she could still remember exactly what he looked like.

Yes, I remember Jordan, she silently answered Mrs. Myston. She'd spent the past few years trying *not* to think about him, alternating between hoping he would be there whenever she came home for vacation, and praying that she'd never have to face him and listen to his taunts again. She hadn't even been home a full twenty-four hours and Mrs. Myston was asking her if she remembered him.

Mrs. Myston continued. "But for some reason he seems to leave the puppy there an awful lot."

"So this is Jordan Sanders' dog?" Maddy asked, glancing at the puppy who was happily digging in an empty flower bed.

"Um-hmm, and I wish he'd take it away from here. I've been chasing this little mischief-maker out of my yard for the last two weeks." Mrs. Myston smoothed a lock of silvery white hair away from her face, leaving a smudge of dark earth on her maple-colored forehead.

"Well, I guess I'll take him over there now. Sorry about your flowers, Mrs. Myston."

"I'll get over it, Madison."

Maddy smiled inwardly. For as long as she could remember, Mrs. Myston had insisted on calling everyone by their full name because she absolutely detested nicknames.

Maddy waved good-bye to the woman and beckoned for the puppy to follow her. "The party's over, Muddy. I'm taking you home."

"Just hope he doesn't think your yard is his new playground," Mrs. Myston said as she got down on her knees to continue working.

As Maddy stepped into the street, she turned around to make sure the puppy was still behind her. "Muddy, you shouldn't make life so hard for Mrs. Myston," she scolded. "She'd probably be really nice if you left her flowers alone." Maddy smiled as an old memory came back to her. "Although, I will admit that I used to get into a lot of trouble with her when I was younger. There's just something about her flower beds that makes you want to reach in and pick a few. But you're going to have to get your habit under control, otherwise—"

Maddy's speech was cut short as a dark blue SUV sped up the street and suddenly stopped in front of her house. The driver's side door opened and a very handsome man whom she instantly recognized as Jordan Sanders jumped out and looked straight at her. His shoulders had gotten a little broader and his skin was darker due to the sun, but everything else was the same.

Maddy's heart fluttered like it had back in high school whenever she'd seen him. *For once it looks like I have Jordan's total attention,* she thought to herself.

"Where do you think you're going with my dog?" he asked abruptly as he stepped over to scoop up the puppy.

Maybe not his full attention, she thought. Maddy turned around and looked for the dognapper. Then she realized he was talking to her. "Excuse me?"

"I said, where are you taking my dog?" His forehead was wrinkled in accusation, and his crescent-shaped eyes narrowed to slits.

Maddy inhaled and exhaled while contemplating an answer. Putting her hands on her hips, she said, "For your information, I found your little troublemaker on my back porch. He left his muddy paw prints on our back door and on my legs. In spite of that, I attempted to do the honorable thing by trying to find his owner. I took him across the street and while I was asking Mrs. Myston if she knew who he belonged to, he proceeded to dig up her flowers. At this very moment, I was taking him to your house, when you jumped out of your car and accused me of trying to steal him. If that's the thanks I get, then I'm sorry I didn't leave him on my back steps, whining and barking."

Jordan shifted from one foot to another. Several moments passed while he stared at her. Maddy grew uncomfortable, realizing he was probably thinking up one of his famous one-liners. The puppy whimpered and struggled to get down, but Jordan acted as though he didn't hear him. Mrs. Myston had abandoned any and all semblance of gardening and was now watching the confrontation with an amused look on her face.

Finally he opened his mouth and retorted, "For your information, this is my parents' house."

"Whatever, Jordan," said Maddy as she walked toward her house.

"Do I know you?" he asked, sounding confused.

Maddy rolled her eyes without even turning around. Her pride had just received a considerable blow, but if he didn't remember her, she wasn't going to make matters worse by trying to jog his memory. *What would I say?* she thought. *You remember. . .I live next door. You used to tease me and call me Madison the Librarian because I made good grades. When I was a sophomore and you were a senior, you told all your friends on the basketball team that I had a crush on you. They started writing me secret admirer notes that appeared to be from you, and when I approached you about it, everybody had a good laugh at my expense. I cried for a week. Now do you remember me?*

"No way am I bringing any of that up," Maddy grumbled. That particular memory never failed to sting a little, even a full six years later.

Just as she opened the front door, Jordan spoke up again. "Hey," he said, a note of surprise coloring his voice.

Maddy gathered up all of her courage and turned to look at him. A look of realization was spreading across his face.

"Madison?" he said, sounding very puzzled. He put the puppy down and jogged across her yard toward the door.

Maddy was flustered. *What does he want now? Is he really about to start teasing me again, after all this time?* Just as Jordan began walking up the porch steps, she slammed the door.

two

Maddy sat down on the floor, put her hand over her mouth and listened as Jordan rang the doorbell repeatedly. Right now she was about half a second away from a good cry. She'd been rude, and he probably felt pretty silly, but she didn't know what else to do. If nothing else, Mrs. Myston was probably being entertained.

She knew she couldn't ignore the ringing doorbell. Her conscience was pricking her and she realized she had to do something. She stood up and opened the door. Jordan stood on the porch, his finger still on the doorbell. He cleared his throat and shifted his weight back and forth. Maddy had never seen him look so unconfident. She glanced across the street and, sure enough, Mrs. Myston was unashamedly still watching.

"Um, Madison, I mean, Maddy, I. . .didn't recognize you. You must be taller or something. And you don't have your glasses anymore."

Maddy arched her eyebrows, waiting for the punch line. Confusion flickered in his fudge-colored eyes.

Jordan put his hand up, as if to stop her from saying anything. "Not that glasses are a bad thing. I wear contacts, myself. So. . ."

"So?" Maddy said, waiting for him to finish.

"So. . .well. . . ." Jordan shrugged and remained quiet.

"So. . .you're telling me that you can't make up the rest of the joke. Is that it?"

"No. . .Maddy, let me explain. I wasn't very mature back then, and I—" The phone began ringing.

"I'd better get that," said Maddy, reaching out to shut the door.

Jordan held out his hand to stop her. "Are you expecting an important call?" he asked.

"Well. . .maybe," Maddy hedged.

"Then I'll wait for you to answer it," he said in his usual confident voice.

Maddy opened her mouth to tell him to just come back later, but the strong set of his jaw told her he was determined to wait, so she hesitantly left the door open and walked into the living room to answer the phone. *I don't care if it's the wrong number. It's an important call as far as I'm concerned,* she decided.

"Hello?"

"Yes, my name is Arnold and I'm calling from American Best Long Distance Company," the voice said.

A sales call. Disappointed, Maddy hesitated, trying to decide what to do.

"Hello?" the man said again.

Maddy glanced toward the front door where Jordan was still waiting. *This is too convenient.* She smiled broadly. "Arnold!" she said happily. "I'm so glad you called." She smiled and paused, hoping it would appear to Jordan that this was an important call.

"Ma'am?" said Arnold, sounding puzzled.

"Arnold, would you hang on just a minute?" she asked pleasantly. "Someone is waiting for me at the door—"

"Excuse me?"

Maddy ignored his comment and continued. "No, no. . .no one important." She emphasized the last word and looked at Jordan, who was listening very carefully. "Just give me a second and I'll be right back." Maddy put the phone down and walked to the door.

"It looks like I need to take that call," she said.

"I guess so. I'll come back later," said Jordan.

Maddy just smiled. "Yes, that would probably be best for me."

"And Arnold, apparently," said Jordan.

"Who?" said Maddy, puzzled.

"On the phone," said Jordan.

"Oh, yes, Arnold. He's probably wondering what happened to me," she said.

"Then I'll come back later," said Jordan.

"You do that," Maddy muttered under her breath as she shut the door.

Relieved, she sat down on the floor once again and breathed a sigh of relief. "Saved by the bell," she murmured. Then she remembered Arnold. Maddy jumped up and ran to the phone, trying to figure out a way to explain all this to him. Hopefully she wouldn't have to change her parents' long distance provider just to make it up to him. When she reached the phone, she found that Arnold had hung up.

She chuckled. "I'll have to keep that technique in mind the next time someone calls trying to sell something I'm not interested in," she said.

She thought about Jordan again, and the tears she'd been trying to hold back started flowing from sheer emotional overload. Then the phone rang again. "Oh, no," said Maddy. Apparently Arnold didn't give up easily.

Maddy shut off her tears and picked up the phone. "Listen, Arnold, I can explain," she said in a rush.

"Um, Maddy, who's Arnold?" She recognized the voice of her older sister Stacy.

"Oh, never mind, it's a long story."

"If you say so. You sound upset. Is everything okay?"

"Give me a few minutes to decide and I'll let you know," said Maddy.

"Okay. . . .So how's the new graduate?"

"Fine. Exactly like I was when you came to my graduation. How's the newlywed?" she asked.

"Maddy, it's been almost five months. I'm not exactly a newlywed anymore," said Stacy.

"I personally would consider five years newlywed since you did promise to spend the rest of your lives together," said Maddy.

"What's five measly months versus the rest of your life?"

"Whatever you say." Stacy laughed. "I'm not up for any philosophical arguments right now."

"Hmm. . .well, since you insist the honeymoon is over, is there anything I should know about?"

"I never said the honeymoon was over, so what in the world are you talking about?"

"Do I have to spell it out? I don't have a summer job yet, so if I need to start buying presents for say, a niece or a nephew. . .I'll need a little advance notice, if you get my drift." Maddy smiled.

"No babies on the way, if that's what you're referring to." Stacy laughed. Then she grew serious. "But enough small talk. What's this Arnold business? And why do you sound like you've been crying?"

"What makes you think I've been crying?" Maddy tried to sound more cheerful.

"The same way I always know you've been crying. Your voice is all croaky. You sound like a frog."

"Thanks a lot, Stacy."

"So what's going on?" Stacy was insistent.

"I don't even know where to start." Maddy's voice began to waver.

"Then don't start now. Why don't you come over for dinner? Max is out of town on business and won't get back until tomorrow. Meanwhile, I'm desperate for company."

"Okay, that sounds like fun," said Maddy. "Just give me a few minutes to freshen up. I've got mud all over my legs, and I need a quick shower."

"Mud?" asked Stacy.

"I told you it's a long story, and you'll hear the whole thing when I get over there."

"I can't wait," said Stacy.

Maddy quickly got some clothes together and was just about to jump in the shower when the phone rang again.

"Hello?" she said.

"Maddy, it's me," said her mother. "Are you really hungry right now, or can your dad and I get a little more shopping done?"

"Hi, Mom. Shop all you want because I'm going to Stacy's for dinner."

"Oh. In that case, we might catch a movie or something."

"That's fine. Do you mind if I take the car?"

"Go right ahead. Oh, and Maddy, I forgot to tell you. Sometimes the Sanders' puppy gets loose and sits on our porch. He can get pretty noisy, and I didn't want you to think he was an intruder. All you have to do is call them and they'll come get him."

"Don't worry, Mom. It already happened and I handled it just fine," she told her. Inwardly, she winced, dreading the thought of having to face Jordan again.

❧

"You played like you knew the phone salesman?" Stacy howled with laughter as Maddy related the events of the afternoon. The two of them were sitting on the couch in Stacy's family room before dinner.

"Well, I had no choice," Maddy said, failing to find it all quite so funny. "It was either stand there and be ridiculed again like in high school or find an excuse to make him leave."

"So what do you think he was going to say?"

Maddy shrugged. "Obviously nothing nice. He had that look on his face."

Stacy rolled her eyes playfully. "What look?"

"The look he always had when he was making fun of me. You know, the 'Maddy's-from-Mars-all-she-ever-does-is-read' look."

Stacy looked sheepish. "You remember all that stuff he used to say?"

"Yes, I do. Don't you?"

"Not really. I was already away at college by that time. All I really remember about Jordan is that he was the bad little kid who lived next door. I think he was a freshman when I was senior."

"But you knew that I had a crush on him for years. Even when I was in the second grade."

"Well, yeah. How could I not know? But you told me you were over that by the time he graduated and left for college. Besides, how can you fall in love in the second grade?"

Maddy rolled her eyes. "Okay, you have a point there. But I had a crush on him all through high school, too."

"But when was the last time you saw him?" Stacy pressed.

Maddy shrugged. "I think two or three years ago. I was home on Christmas break." She wished Stacy would stop probing now, because she didn't want to admit what she thought she was feeling.

Stacy leaned forward. "You still like him? You haven't even seen him in two or three years."

Maddy grew defensive. "Of course not. But I am curious about what he's been doing since I last saw him."

Stacy put her hand on her forehead and reclined back on the couch. "If you don't like him, then why are you so interested in what he's been doing?"

"I can't be curious about my neighbor?"

"You can be curious about your neighbor, but I don't think it's wise to be curious about an old crush who has a history of making fun of you."

"I guess you're right." Maddy was quiet for a moment, reflecting on what Stacy had said. It made perfect sense, but she was having a hard time ignoring all that had occurred. Then, she remembered something else. "Stacy, he didn't even recognize me!"

"So?"

"So?" Maddy stood up and did an imitation of a model on a runway. "That means I must look totally different to him."

"Is that a good thing?" Stacy lifted her eyebrows.

Maddy sat down, discouraged. "You are no fun, you know that?"

A timer went off in the kitchen. "What did you want me to say?" Stacy stood up. "I think the pasta's done. Come on in the kitchen and help me with the rest of dinner."

Maddy frowned. "Are you kidding? You know I don't cook. I'll wait right here for you."

Stacy playfully put her hands on her hips. "Shall I refresh your memory with the story of the Little Red Hen? Or do you want me to paraphrase my point directly from Scripture: If you don't work, you don't eat."

Maddy folded her arms. "Then I'll order pizza."

Stacy sighed. "Forget it. Just come in here and talk to me, at least," Stacy said, beckoning Maddy to follow her.

Maddy stood up slowly. "Fine. If you insist, Betty Crocker," she said sarcastically. "But the second you ask me to stir something, I'm back in the family room."

"Lord help the man you marry," said Stacy, as she opened a jar of spaghetti sauce.

"I'm not planning on getting married any time soon. I have a great career ahead of me, and when I do get married, I'm not going to be some man's cook, or laundry woman, or gardener, or secretary. We'll be equal partners," Maddy shot back.

"You can only be equal partners if you are willing to do things equally," Stacy said quietly.

"What are you implying?"

"I'm not implying. I'm saying that Max and I are equal partners, but we both cook. We both do laundry. We both do errands for each other. We're not experts at everything. He's better at laundry and I'm a better cook. You don't cook or do laundry. You don't have many domestic skills. How can you expect to be equal?"

Maddy frowned. Stacy could be so frustratingly bossy sometimes. The bad thing was, she was making a lot of sense right now. "Mom and Dad don't care," she retorted.

Stacy shook her head. "No, they just gave up after you flunked home ec."

"So? That was the only time I flunked anything. I made

straight A's in all my math and science classes. Even physics and calculus."

"They just figured you would eventually come around. But I know Mom's concerned about it."

"Enough." Maddy put her hands over her ears. "I know I need to learn someday. And I will. Just not now."

Stacy shrugged.

Maddy grew uncomfortable because Stacy looked smug. But they had pretty much called a truce and she didn't want to push things, so she changed the subject. "So are you going to tell me what Jordan's been doing lately?"

"As far as I know, he graduated from art school in New Jersey a couple years ago. There was something about him almost getting kicked out of school, but I guess that all got cleared up."

"Kicked out? Who told you that?"

"Mrs. Myston. But I didn't let her go into all of the details. You know how she can get. Plus, I don't think she knew the whole story. I guess his parents didn't want to discuss it, and she was asking me if I knew what happened."

"Oh." Maddy understood. If Mrs. Myston didn't know the whole story, she would ask around until she found out. Maddy was actually a little surprised Mrs. Myston hadn't asked her about it. "So then what happened?" she asked Stacy.

"Then I heard he moved to New York and worked, but then decided to move back here six or seven months ago. I think he started his own business."

"Really? What does he do?"

"I don't know. Art, I guess. Someone told me he paints murals for people."

Now Maddy lifted her eyebrows. "Hmm, you seem to be on top of things. How do you know about this?"

"Well, Mrs. Myston told me about the college thing. And one of my clients who got married about two or three months ago filled me in on the rest. We were at the rehearsal and I asked if she knew who painted the murals on the walls in the hallways. She told me it was one of the guys who went to church there, and she mentioned his name. I told her he used to live next door to me, and she told me what I just told you."

"So Jordan goes to church now? Are you telling me he's a Christian?"

"I don't know. I assumed he was. And if you're even remotely interested in him, you'd better make sure he is before you start getting all emotionally entangled."

"Stacy." Maddy was sarcastic. "You sound like Mom." She paused, then continued. "Of course I'm not going to date a guy who's not a Christian."

"I just wanted to make sure before this whole thing went too far," Stacy said apologetically.

Maddy nodded and was silent a few moments. Then she spoke up again. "Stacy?"

"Yeeeessss?" Stacy singsonged, then sighed. "This subject is getting boring to me so let's wrap it up soon, okay?"

"Okay. My question is: Do you think I look prettier than I did in high school?"

"Maddy, you've always looked pretty to me. Since the day they brought you home from the hospital. A little wrinkly, but still pretty."

"No, Stacy, this is important. Don't give me a 'sister' answer. Tell me from a non-relative point of view."

"Okay." Stacy took a deep breath and looked at Maddy for a few minutes. "I guess the contacts make a difference. And. . . you're not so skinny anymore. You've gotten kind of curvy in the right places. But you're still short." Stacy's voice took on a teasing tone. "I hate to break it you, but I don't think you'll ever hit five feet. You're still about half an inch too short."

"And I wear makeup every once in a while, and I don't wear jeans and tennis shoes every day," Maddy finished. "I even own a few dresses that I like to wear."

"Yeah, I guess. So is this about Jordan?"

"Kind of. I think I was somewhat of a tomboy when I was

younger. And in high school I was a total bookworm. So now maybe I've just blossomed, and Jordan finally sees me as a woman, instead of the skinny girl with glasses who lives next door and always has a book with her."

"Maybe he does, Maddy, but there's nothing wrong with any of those things. You were beautiful back then too. Jordan just didn't notice, so it was his loss, not yours."

"That's what you think."

"Fine," Stacy laughed. "Have it your way. But I'll tell you something else that used to get Jordan's attention."

"What?" Maddy smiled.

"Cookies. Homemade. The way to that man's heart was definitely through his stomach. Now tell me how you intend to remedy that? I think he might be a better cook than you."

"I don't need to remedy the situation. I see it as a perfect match. He'll cook, and I'll wash the dishes."

"Is that so?" Stacy teased.

"Yeah." Maddy wiggled her eyebrows up and down and stuck her tongue out.

"Then I'll let you brush up on your dishwashing skills after dinner."

Both women burst into giggles.

"But I'm warning you," said Maddy. "Don't use your best china unless you have rubber floors. You know I hold the record for the most broken dishes."

three

Jordan Sanders sat in his parents' living room and looked out the window for probably the fifteenth time in fifteen minutes. He couldn't believe the beautiful woman he'd inadvertently started an argument with was Madison Thompson. Madison the midget, he'd called her in high school. That and a host of other names. He grimaced at the thought. She had grown maybe an inch since high school, but he was still well over a foot taller. Who would have guessed she'd turn out to be so. . . gorgeous?

Jordan closed his eyes and tried to remember what it was about her that had first caught his attention this afternoon. Everything. Her smooth, glowing skin reminded him of pure honey mixed with shimmering gold dust. Madison's round face was gently framed by dark, glossy hair that just brushed her shoulders and moved as gracefully as she did. Her hazel eyes had grown fiery and bright when she'd fussed at him about the puppy. He didn't remember ever noticing her eyes before. As he stood on her porch and tried to apologize, it seemed like she'd turned to stone. Her wide eyes grew cool, and he searched her round face in hopes of seeing the tiniest trace of emotion somewhere. He hadn't been one hundred percent sure, but he thought her eyes seemed to be unusually wet, and it tore at his heart to think he might have made her cry. When had she stopped being the wiry kid with the glasses who had followed him around adoringly and blossomed into the woman with the round lips, softly curving figure, and the chip on her shoulder?

Five years ago, she'd had a huge crush on him. When he would leave on the weekends to go on dates, he would sometimes see her peeking out of a window. He hadn't cared back then and had laughed at her. Girls had lined up to go out with him, and Maddy had hardly been his type.

Now the tables had turned. Not only had he waited for her to come back so long he had missed the singles' Bible study at his church, but he was also literally staring out his window waiting for her return. She'd left over two hours ago; he'd told her he was coming back over. She obviously didn't care. It was a Friday evening and she was probably out on a date with Arnold, laughing at him.

I wonder how serious she and Arnold are? he thought.

"Jordan?" His mother called.

"I'm in the living room," he answered.

"Are you staying for dinner?" His mother entered the room and looked at him. "Are you okay? Why don't you turn the lights on?"

Jordan shook his head and stood up. "No, Mom, I don't think so. And I'm feeling fine. I'm just really tired."

"Well. . ." His mother stared at him doubtfully. "Are you sure? I made collard greens. . .and your dad and I can't eat them all. Why don't you take some home?"

"Nah, I'm not too hungry. But I'll probably be back tomorrow."

"Two days in a row? I might just have to bake a cake for you," she laughed. "To what do I owe this honor?"

He leaned down and kissed her on the cheek. "Mom, you act like I never come to visit. I'm here once or twice a week."

"I know. We just get lonely for you sometimes."

"Okay, okay. You'll see me tomorrow, and thanks again for keeping the puppy for me."

"You're welcome, but I have to tell you that dog gets into more trouble. It's only been a couple weeks, but the neighbors are starting to get upset. The next time you decide to impulsively buy a dog, please make sure there aren't any rules against having pets where you live."

Jordan sighed. "I'm really sorry about that, Mom. I hope

he's not too much trouble for you and Dad. I'll be moving to a new apartment in another month or so, and then I'll take him with me."

His mother sighed dramatically. "Of course, we really don't mind having him around. Especially since he's the closest thing to a grandchild we have right now. We'll just shower all of our grandparently love on him for the time being."

Jordan laughed heartily. "Mom, I don't think 'grandparently' is a real word."

"Of course it isn't." She laughed. "I just needed to come up with something fast, and 'grandparently' was the only word I could think of to get my point across."

Jordan chuckled. "I've got to get home, but how about you and dad joining me at church on Sunday? We could go for brunch afterwards."

His mother sighed. "Honey, you know I'm glad that your religion seems to have helped you through. . .some difficult times in your life, but it's not for me right now. And you know how it upsets your father when you mention your being—" Jordan figured she was probably trying to think of a word besides "fanatical" as his dad liked to say. After several moments, she looked back toward the kitchen where his father was. With a pleading look in her eye, she shrugged. "You know what I mean," she said, lowering her voice.

Jordan lifted his eyebrows. "Saved?" he asked, vocalizing the word she couldn't bring herself to say. It was frustrating not being able to comfortably discuss his Christianity with his family.

His mother spoke slowly. "If that's what you want to call it. But, no, we won't be coming with you to church. We can still do the brunch if you'd like." She smiled hopefully.

Jordan's heart sank. This was the way it always went. If he invited his father to church, the conversation erupted into a bellowing lecture from his dad about Jordan being weak. If he asked his mother, she politely refused, citing that religion was 'not for her.'

Jordan walked to the door. "I'll let you know, okay? And please say good night to the puppy for me."

"We will. And Jordan?"

He turned around, ready to answer her question. "Yeah?"

"It would be nice if you would give the dog a name. We hate to go around just calling him 'puppy.' "

Jordan slapped his hand to his forehead. "I keep forgetting. I'll try to come up with something this week, okay?" He waved good-bye and headed out to his car, noting that no one seemed to be at home next door.

ൠ

The next morning, Jordan got up bright and early, in order to stop by Maddy's before he went to work. On his way there, he stopped by the grocery store and bought a card. As an afterthought, he also purchased a single yellow rose. He'd heard yellow roses symbolized friendship, and he wanted to give Maddy a token of peace. He pulled in front of her house, hoping his parents didn't get upset that he hadn't stopped in to see them first. As he walked up the driveway, he took a deep breath, hoping she would be in a better mood today.

He rang the doorbell and waited. Nothing happened, so he rang it again. Maybe they were all asleep. It was just a couple of minutes after seven, but it was also a Saturday morning. He'd hoped they might at least be stirring around. Apparently, they were still sleeping. Or maybe not. He fidgeted nervously and wondered if Maddy was still too upset to talk to him. For all he knew, she could be looking through the peephole and laughing at him. He shrugged and started walking toward his car.

He knew in his heart he was sorry for the way he'd acted years ago, and God knew, too. If Maddy didn't want to hear his apology, then the Lord would just have to heal her heart without Jordan's help.

He'd only taken three steps away from the porch when he heard the front door swing open. Jordan turned to see Mrs.

Thompson standing at the door in a fluffy periwinkle robe with a puzzled look on her face.

She covered her mouth to mask a yawn. "Jordan?" Mrs. Thompson blinked several times.

He cleared his throat. "Hi, Mrs. Thompson. Is Maddy home? I just wanted to talk to her for a second."

Berniece looked at him with a sharp expression on her face. He knew the look. It was a look of distrust, and he didn't blame her. He wouldn't trust himself either, if he were Maddy's mother or father.

They had politely endured his mischievous antics in grade school, and at that time had even been somewhat friendly to his parents. But when his high school years rolled around, which included his endless teasing of Maddy and the parade of girlfriends he collected, her parents had even stopped speaking to his parents, except for the customary neighborly wave and 'hello' and 'good-bye.'

He knew for a fact that since he and Maddy had gone to college, their parents had been able to take steps toward a friendship once again, although his parents complained that the Thompsons were too religious. He'd secretly been hoping that the Thompsons might be able to convince his parents to take steps toward salvation, and now he wondered if he might be messing things up again. It would hardly come as a shock to him if Maddy's mother decided to chew him out right here and now. He looked across the street. *And wouldn't you know it, Mrs. Myston is working in her flower beds at this hour of the morning,* he thought.

Beginning back when he was in the fourth grade and had developed a habit of running through her flower beds and immaculate yard, Mrs. Myston had warned Jordan about his getting a comeuppance for his deeds someday. However, that particular bad habit had ended by the ninth grade. But by then, she'd switched from harping about her yard to lecturing him about his reputation for having a different girlfriend every week or so. And though he never admitted it to her, the thought of being punished worried him, because punishment was something he heard about only from other kids or saw parents dish out to their children on television sitcoms.

Most adults and even some of his peers said he was spoiled because he was an only child, and not only did he agree with that, but he was proud of the fact. He had no siblings with which to play and therefore had no need to ever share anything. For the first seven or eight years of his life, he'd begged and pleaded for a little sister or brother, and his parents bought him toys to make up for the missing siblings. By the time he accepted the fact he would always be an only child, he decided it was for the best. He was the sole beneficiary of his parents' total attention, both emotional and monetary.

On occasion, he felt touches of loneliness, but there were always plenty of kids at any given time who were more than willing to put up with his selfishness and moodiness in order to play with his multitude of toys. When they grew too old for toys, the same kids wanted to ride in his new car, and girls didn't mind being seen with a guy who had a huge wardrobe of expensive clothing. And although he'd never had to share anything in his life, he'd learned that it paid to use his generous allowance to buy flowers and gifts for his dates. Back then, he never gave without the intention of being paid back.

He scratched his head and thought about Mrs. Myston again. He hadn't thought about her warnings in a long time, and he had pretty much gotten over the fear of what his punishment might be. But as it looked, in a matter of minutes, he *was* going to get his comeuppance. Mrs. Myston, who'd predicted there was going to be such retribution, had seen the first of it yesterday and would be fortunate enough to see part two this morning.

Mrs. Thompson looked beyond him and waved to Mrs. Myston. Then, to his surprise, she opened the door wider and waved him in. "I guess we overslept a little today, but I'll run up and see if Maddy is awake. Why don't you come in and wait in the living room."

Jordan hurried inside and stood in the entry hall, trying to think of something to say. For the second time in two days, he was speechless, and that in and of itself was somewhat terrifying. He'd lived most of his life possessing a back pocket full of quick, although not always polite, comebacks to everyone.

The more he'd let Jesus into his thought life, the more these answers seemed to evade him, which was a little refreshing sometimes, except when he was standing in someone's front entry hall, his mind racing, but leaving his mouth at a loss for words. Mrs. Thompson looked down at the card and flower he held, reminding him that he still held them.

"It's for Maddy," was the only thing he could think of to say.

"Oh," she said, lifting her eyebrows slightly. When he didn't answer, but merely nodded his head, she pointed toward the living room and said, "Why don't you go in there and have a seat. I'll go get Maddy." As he started to move to the living room, she turned and went up the stairs.

Jordan sat down on the oversized ivory sofa and looked around. He didn't remember actually ever having been inside the Thompsons' house. The color scheme consisted mainly of different shades of white complemented with varying hues of green, ranging from celadon to forest green. He suddenly felt underdressed and wished he'd worn something besides his old jeans and T-shirt. Soon after he'd started art school and began to focus on his painting rather than dating, he'd given up expensive clothing in favor of clothes he could actually work in.

Still, it was a little unnerving to be on such unfamiliar turf wearing clothes that were really only suitable for getting paint splattered on them. He wished Maddy would just come downstairs so he could apologize and get it over with. *I wonder what's taking her so long?*

The thought occurred to him that Mrs. Thompson might have gone to get her husband to yell at him instead of going to wake Maddy. He guessed he probably deserved it. He also remembered his clothes had several paint stains on them and he began to wonder if somehow, the stains might have gotten on the furniture. He quickly stood up and checked the sofa. It was as clean as a whistle. Just to be on the safe side, he decided to remain standing while he waited.

After almost ten minutes, he decided she wasn't going to come down and talk to him. And it didn't seem like anyone was going to inform him of Maddy's decision, either. They were going to let him sweat it out. And he was already starting to do so.

Then an idea hit him. He could just leave the card and flower and she would see it when she was good and ready. He sat the items on the end table next to the sofa and headed toward the front door. However, he underestimated the distance between his foot and the table leg, and as he turned to walk away, he tripped over the small round table, knocking it over, along with the phone that had rested on the tabletop and the items he'd just placed there.

At least they have wall-to-wall carpeting, Jordan thought. The table had merely made a muffled *thump,* but the phone seemed to fall a bit harder. Or it could have seemed loud only because he was so nervous. Jordan looked around, expecting one of the Thompsons to come running in. When they didn't, he set the table upright, and placed the phone back on top. This was the same phone Maddy had picked up yesterday when Arnold called. As he put his card and the now-beginning-to-wilt rose back on the table, he wondered about Arnold. *What kind of name is Arnold, anyway? Somehow, I can't imagine Maddy being stuck with some guy named Arnold.* He shook the thoughts away. It was time to get out of here. He'd done his job. *So why am I standing here, staring at the Thompsons' phone, wondering what kind of guy Maddy's boyfriend is?*

"Ahem."

Jordan looked up and saw Maddy standing in the entrance

of the room. She looked even prettier than she had yesterday, wearing a long turquoise sundress that complemented her brown skin. Now he realized why she'd taken so long. How thoughtless of him to barge in on a woman first thing in the morning. No way was she going to jump out of bed and run downstairs to see the man who'd made fun of her personal appearance for years.

He wished there was a way for him to tell her how attractive she was without putting her on the defensive or making her suspicious that he was up to something underhanded.

He took a deep breath and smiled. "I was beginning to wonder if you were going to come."

She smiled back, looking much more at ease than she had yesterday. "And I was beginning to wonder how our phone found its way to the floor."

"Oh." If it was possible for a man to blush, Jordan figured he would fit into that category at this moment. "I was just about to leave when I accidentally knocked the table over," he explained. "I didn't hear you coming."

Maddy laughed. Her laugh was as refreshing as a cool breeze, in contrast to the reception he'd been expecting. "I guess not, considering all of the noise you were making knocking things over."

"Sorry," was all Jordan said. *If only I could stop sweating,* he thought, as he reached up and casually wiped his forehead. Somehow, it felt strange for her to be teasing him. He was here, after all, to apologize for his own teasing. *Can't she cut me a little slack?* He wiped his forehead one more time, and hoped she didn't notice.

"Well, here I am," she said cheerfully. "You look a little warm. Is it too hot in here? We could go outside."

Jordan looked toward the front door and thought about Mrs. Myston who was probably waiting for him to get tossed out on his ear. He'd rather pour sweat in the Thompsons' living room than have Mrs. Myston witness what might be ahead. He shook his head. "I'm okay."

"Are you sure? We could go out to the sunroom. There aren't any gardening neighbors out there," she said.

Jordan laughed. This might not be so hard after all. Maddy had a pretty healthy sense of humor. And she apparently understood his not wanting Mrs. Myston to see and hear what he had to say. "The sunroom sounds great," he said.

Maddy turned and led the way past the family room, through the kitchen to the sunroom. Her parents were sitting in the breakfast nook, and when he smiled at them, they managed to smile back.

The entrance to the sunroom was in the kitchen. The back wall of the kitchen was a series of glass panels and even though the kitchen and sunroom were two separate rooms, they were separated only by a wall of glass. He sighed, realizing he'd jumped from the frying pan into the fire. He didn't know what was worse, Mrs. Myston or Mr. and Mrs. Thompson. He swallowed hard and had the fleeting thought that the lump he'd just forced down was probably his pride. He stopped in the middle of the kitchen. Maddy opened the door to the sunroom and waited for him to follow.

Jordan stood his ground. *Since I have to do it, I might as well do it right,* he decided. "Actually, I can say what I have to say right here." Mr. and Mrs. Thompson looked at him with surprise and expectancy on their faces. He wiped his forehead again. Maybe he'd spoken too soon. He felt another lump build in his throat. Pride was a stubborn pill to swallow.

"We don't mind you using the sunroom," said Mrs. Thompson. She looked like she felt a little sorry for him.

"No." Jordan put his hands up to quell any further arguments. He made eye contact with Maddy and started talking before he lost his nerve. "Maddy, I just came over to apologize to you and your family about the way I used to tease you. I could make an excuse and say I didn't know better, but that wouldn't be the whole truth. My parents let me get away with a lot, but I knew in my heart that I was hurting your feelings. I became a Christian about three years ago and I knew the Lord didn't appreciate what I'd done." He shrugged. "I'm just sorry it took me so long to tell you." He quickly strode over to Maddy and handed her the flower and the card. She looked stunned. "And I'm sorry I yelled at you about my dog yesterday. I'd had a bad day at work, but it didn't make my actions right."

Maddy looked at the card and then at him.

"It—it's not a love note or anything," he stuttered. "I just wanted to write down how sorry I was and how I hope you'll forgive me."

Maddy nodded and solemnly said, "I forgive you."

Jordan sighed in relief. It was done. Except it felt like something in his heart had suddenly opened when she'd spoken to him. She had allowed him to come into her home and in spite of the past had managed to sincerely treat him with trust and understanding. With a sudden rush of unexplainable emotion, his heart felt relieved of a burden. *She's the one,* he thought.

Jordan pushed the thought away as he grew aware of an awkward silence that had settled in the room. It would be best for him to leave, but. . .he knew he had to do something in order to see her again. Only, with the apology being complete, he had absolutely no reason to see her again.

The reality of that thought was not very appealing. He took what felt like his hundredth deep breath in the last ten minutes and decided to plunge ahead and say what he felt like saying before he lost the nerve. "We don't have to talk ever again if you don't want to. But I would like to be your friend. The decision is up to you."

No one said anything. He figured he'd said too much. And he had the feeling he'd sounded incredibly. . .unmasculine. He hurried to get himself out of the hole he'd just dug. "But you don't have to say no or even yes right now. You can think about it, okay?"

"Okay," Maddy said slowly.

"So I guess I'd better go. I'm gonna be late for work," he

said.

"Oh, I'm sorry," said Maddy. "I'll walk you to the door." She led the way and he silently followed. She opened the door and moved aside for him to leave.

He walked to his car feeling confused and a little embarrassed about his impulsive request. Was it asking too much to want not only forgiveness, but also friendship?

Jordan reached his car and opened the door with a heavy heart. Forgiveness was all he'd come for and he'd gotten it. Anything more, he really didn't deserve from her.

As he pulled away, he casually glanced at the doorway and was surprised and encouraged to see her standing in the doorway waving to him. While he returned the wave, he prayed.

Thank you, Lord, for letting her forgive me. And if it's Your will, please let there be a way for me to be her friend. . .and eventually, maybe more.

four

Maddy stood in front of the mirror and eyed her reflection. Nervously, she smoothed nonexistent wrinkles out of her ankle-length, fuchsia matte jersey dress. She hoped she looked professional enough.

Today was her second interview for the position of computer instructor at the Ernst Mevlom day camp for teens who were academically advanced in the field of communications. She'd gone to the first interview during her spring break. During her second semester, she'd kept in touch with the head administrator, Mrs. Calvin, who had nearly promised her the job. This second interview was more of an open house for the board of directors and alumni teachers to meet those who had applied for teaching positions.

Still, she couldn't help but feel a little jittery. *What if they decide I'm not the person they're looking for?* Her sister Stacy had offered her a job working in the wedding planning business, but Maddy had done that last summer and the hours were erratic. Plus, she wanted her weekends to be more free, which was almost impossible in that line of work, since people seemed to always get married on weekends.

Taking deep breaths to calm down, she slipped on a light jacket over the dress and headed outside to her car.

As she put her seat belt on, she heard a tapping on her back window. Looking behind her, she was startled to see Jordan standing behind her car.

She smiled, happy that he'd come over to see her. It had been a little over a week since his apology, and she had been wondering if she'd even get a chance to really thank him. She had figured he had gotten too embarrassed and decided not to come over again.

While she rolled the window down, Jordan walked around to her side of the car.

Maddy grinned. "I wondered if I'd see you again."

Jordan leaned down and looked into the car. "Well. . .I thought you might need a little time to think about it," he said. He smiled.

"So do you think nine days was enough time?" Maddy said in a teasing tone.

He lifted an eyebrow and said, "Why don't you tell me?"

"Hmm. . . ," said Maddy. She paused and waited to see his reaction.

Jordan's smile disappeared as he stood up and put his hands in his pockets.

"Actually, five minutes was enough time," replied Maddy. "I know it took a lot of courage for you to apologize like that, and I really appreciated it. And if the offer still stands, I can always use a friend."

"You're not just saying that?" asked Jordan.

Maddy shook her head. "No, I might have been pretty upset with you, but I wouldn't joke about something like that."

He grinned and playfully exaggerated wiping his brow.

Maddy cleared her throat and looked at her watch. It was a little after 8:30. "I hate to ruin this friendly moment and all, but I need to be somewhere in about twenty minutes, so. . . ," she trailed off, not quite knowing how she should end the conversation.

"Hey, sorry about that. I've actually got to be somewhere, too. But if you're not busy later on, do you want to get together and do something tonight?"

Maddy's eyes widened. "Are you asking me out?"

He shrugged. "I guess so."

Maddy tilted her head to the side and lifted an eyebrow. "In what sense?"

"What do you mean?"

"In what sense are you asking me out? As in a date or as friends?"

Jordan considered for a few seconds. "As friends. Is that acceptable?"

Maddy smiled halfheartedly. "Sure. What time?"

"Is eight o'clock okay?"

"Yeah. Where are we going?"

"Actually, I don't know. This is all off the top of my head."

"Oh, really?"

"Um-hmm, but here's what we'll do. I'll tell you what I thought of tonight, and if you don't like my idea, you can pick something. Deal?"

"Deal." Maddy turned the key to start the ignition. "Now if you'll excuse me, I have to get to an interview."

Jordan stepped back to allow her room to leave. "I'll be praying for your interview to go well," he said.

"I can use it." Maddy laughed as she backed out of the driveway.

On her way to the interview, she replayed the scene between her and Jordan in her memory. She was happy about seeing Jordan again, but something about the whole conversation was gnawing at her thoughts. She really had figured he wouldn't come back, and she had even considered going over to his parents' house to find out how to get in touch with him, but since he'd come back today, she wouldn't have to go that route. And now, Jordan Sanders, her old crush and arch nemesis had asked her out.

Although, she reasoned, *it's only a friendly date.* Maddy frowned. That was the part that bothered her. He had hesitated when she asked if it were a date. Sure, she wanted to be his friend, but her old feelings for him were more apparent, even after years of trying not to dwell on them. *I'd be so hurt if he really just wants to be my friend,* she thought.

Was he only doing this to further make amends for his actions in the past? She didn't want him to start regarding her as a pity case—someone he wouldn't normally be friends with but felt compelled to be nice to.

Maddy shook her head. *He has to feel something,* she told

herself. *I just don't see Jordan Sanders as the type of guy to go out with someone he can't stand.*

As she pulled into the parking lot of the Mevlom Institute, she decided to stop worrying and spend the next few hours focusing on securing her job. As far as Jordan was concerned, she'd think about him later.

❧

Jordan placed the small square of fabric next to the strip of cardboard he'd just finished painting. He squinted for the umpteenth time, trying to determine if the shade of paint he'd just blended matched the fabric sample from his client's sofa. Judge Margaret Wilbrieg had requested a toned-down lime green as the main color of the abstract she'd hired Jordan to paint. So far, the paint stores had been unable to mix a color to suit Judge Wilbrieg's tastes. Jordan had stopped running from store to store and had spent the better part of the morning trying to mix the color himself.

Things were going slower than they probably should have since he'd been thinking about his conversation with Maddy. Was it his imagination or had disappointment shaded her face when he said he was asking her out as a friend? He wasn't sure. But he was inclined to chalk it up to his imagination, due to the fact that she obviously had a serious relationship with that guy Arnold. If anything, she was probably just making sure he had only feelings of friendship for her since she was already dating someone. In all likelihood, she was probably glad she didn't have to inform him that they could only be friends. Why should she be disappointed that he wanted to be just friends if she was happy with Arnold?

He walked around the room slowly, trying to see if the paint sample stayed true to the color of the fabric square in different lighting. As he walked, his thoughts strayed back to Maddy. *Was she really happy with Arnold? Of course she is. Remember the way she smiled when Arnold called her that day? She just accepted my invitation because she wanted to make me feel better about my apology. So we'll just go out as*

*friends, and that'll be the end of it. She has Arnold, and I
don't need to embarrass myself by trying to suggest anything
more than friendship to her.*

At that moment, Judge Wilbrieg walked into the room.
"Jordan, I'm heading to the office, and I'd appreciate it if
you could get that color matched up sometime today. I want
that mural to be done before my annual barbecue, and June
13 is only three weeks away."

Jordan held up the sample he'd been studying. "How does
this look?"

Her eyes widened and she smiled with approval. "That's
perfect. I'm so relieved that we have the color." She walked
to the wall where the mural was to be painted. "I know at
first I wanted it to be abstract, but now I've changed my
mind. I still don't want it to be symmetrical, but maybe a little more sedate. Maybe some big sweeping strokes here, with
a touch of some other color like marine blue or purple to fill
in." She gestured excitedly as she spoke.

Jordan cleared his throat. "Okay. . .but are you sure you
have time? Didn't you say you were heading to work?"

She shrugged. "In a minute, but first, I want to take a look
at the other colors again. I'm really starting to have second
thoughts about the fuchsia."

Jordan sighed and tried to follow her rapid stream of sug-
gestions on how he should paint the wall. Glancing at his
watch, he noted it was just eleven o'clock. He couldn't
remember a day when eight o'clock had seemed so far away.

ও

It was a little after two o'clock when Maddy left the Mevlom
Institute, her stomach growling slightly, and her feet starting to
ache. After she and the other applicants had watched a short
film about the work of the institute, Mrs. Calvin had taken
them on a tour of the massive building. After that came the
informal brunch with the returning staff and the board of
directors. After that, the board retreated to an office to interview each applicant again.

Maddy waited with the others outside the room while each applicant spent an average of half an hour in the interviews. While she waited, she had prayed to keep from getting too nervous. After their interviews, the other applicants each left until Maddy was the fourth and final one to be interviewed. She entered the room and tried her best to answer all the questions flung at her. She thought she had done well. The message she'd hoped to convey was the fact that she really felt she had a lot to offer both the institute and the teens at the Mevlom day camp.

They assured her they were impressed with her, but they had to choose carefully since they had only three positions to offer and four applicants to choose from. When her interview ended, Mrs. Calvin told her she would be contacting all of the applicants later in the day to inform them of the decision.

Maddy inhaled the fresh air, happy to be outside. She hoped she could find a way to occupy her time until she received a phone call from Mrs. Calvin. Hopefully, she would have good news for her. If not, it was back to weddings and those all day work schedules on Saturdays. Maddy concentrated on selecting what she would wear tonight when she went out with Jordan.

When she pulled up to the house, she noticed Mrs. Myston outside in her garden. Jordan's puppy sat in her yard, watching her as she worked. After parking the car, Maddy walked over to Mrs. Myston.

"Hello, Madison," said Mrs. Myston.

"Hello, Mrs. Myston," she answered. Pointing toward the puppy, she remarked, "I see your little friend is back."

Mrs. Myston shook her head in exasperation. "The Sanders aren't home, so I can't get rid of him. Might as well keep an eye on him."

Maddy laughed. "It doesn't look like he's a threat to your garden anymore."

"That's what he wants you to think," replied the older woman. "He's just waiting for me to turn my back so he can undo what I've been doing out here." Mrs. Myston glared at the puppy. The puppy tilted his head to the side and wagged his tail.

Maddy tried to hold back a smile. "So what are you going to do with him after you get done?"

Mrs. Myston shrugged. "I don't plan on leaving him out here, that's for sure. I guess I'll just keep on working until the Sanders get back."

Maddy grew concerned. The air was starting to get warm, and she didn't think it would be too healthy for Mrs. Myston to work in the sun for so long. Mrs. Myston's forehead was beaded with sweat and her skin was looking a little flushed.

Maddy looked at the puppy, and he gazed back at her with brown eyes. He stood up and trotted over to her. He tried to jump up on her legs, but Maddy backed away. This was why she had never wanted a pet. They were too messy. But she couldn't let Mrs. Myston stay outdoors for who knew how long until Jordan or his parents came to claim the puppy.

She took a deep breath and hoped she wouldn't regret what she was going to say. "It's getting pretty hot out here. Why don't you go inside and cool off? I'll watch the puppy for a while."

Mrs. Myston's eyes lit up. "Thank you so much, Madison. I've been out here for almost two hours, and I didn't really know how much longer I could stay out here. I just hated to see my garden get torn up again."

"Well, it's not a problem, really. Since he's not too dirty, I'll just put him in the sunroom until Jordan comes. . . ." Maddy trailed off, realizing she'd inadvertently told Mrs. Myston that Jordan was coming over.

"I guess you and Jordan have everything worked out?" said Mrs. Myston.

Maddy didn't feel like answering a lot of personal questions about her relationship with Jordan. Mostly because there wasn't any relationship to discuss. Jordan had made it clear he wanted only to be her friend. Mrs. Myston would find out soon enough that Jordan wasn't romantically interested in Maddy. "I guess so," she said slowly.

"Going on a date tonight?" Mrs. Myston continued.

"Oh, no. . .just a little friendly get-together. But I should probably get home. I'm waiting to hear the results of an interview I had this morning, and you probably want to take a break."

"It is getting warm out here," Mrs. Myston agreed. "I'll talk to you later, Madison, and I hope you get the job."

"Thanks," said Maddy. She called the puppy and walked back to her house. She didn't want to risk him messing up something, so she led him to the sunroom by way of the backyard.

"Now, you've got to stay in here until Jordan comes," she told him. "And if you break something, don't think I won't make him pay for it." The puppy wagged his tail. When she turned to leave, the puppy started whimpering. *Oh great*, she thought. *A whining puppy is not my idea of a good houseguest.* Maddy sat down and tried to think of a way to get him to be quiet. She had planned to take a short nap, but she didn't think she would be able to tolerate hearing him whimper for the next few hours. Then she noticed that he had grown quiet. "Good," she said, standing up. "I'll be back to check on you in a little while, and I meant what I said about you breaking stuff.

When she opened the door, the puppy started whimpering again. Maddy groaned. "Are you saying you want me to stay here?" The puppy wagged his tail. "I guess I could sit out here for a little while. Just let me go change my clothes." Maddy hurried to her room and changed. Sure enough, even upstairs, she could still hear the puppy loudly protesting the fact that she had left him alone.

On her way back to the sunroom she stopped in her mother's craft room and found her mother stenciling colorful animal designs on a small wooden footstool.

"Mom, I thought you might be in here. What are you up to?" Her mother looked up. "I promised to paint six of these for the church nursery by Sunday."

"They look good so far," Maddy said as she glanced at two that were already finished. "I just got back from my interview, and I'm still waiting on a call to find out if I got the job."

"I'm sure you did fine. But what is that noise?"

"Oh, I volunteered to keep Jordan's puppy out of Mrs. Myston's flower beds until Jordan arrives or his parents get home."

Berniece nodded. "Just make sure you keep him in the sunroom. I saw Jordan stop you on your way out this morning," said Berniece. "Is everything okay?" Her mother's eyes crinkled with concern.

Maddy could hardly contain her smile. "It's better than okay, Mom. He asked me out."

Berniece smiled and looked relieved. "Well, that sounds like fun. I'm glad you two seem to be getting along."

Maddy nodded. "I'm just glad that he came over today. And he says that he's asked me out as a friend, so there's no pressure for us to decide if we really like each other, but I kind of think he might be slightly interested in more than friendship."

"Honey, the best thing I can tell you is to keep the Lord with you every step of the way. He knows how this will all turn out, and if you remember to ask Him before you make your decisions, He won't let you take a wrong turn." Berniece dipped her paintbrush in a container of water and swished it around.

"I know, Mom," Maddy said. She leaned over and kissed her mother's cheek. "But I've got to get back to that puppy before someone cites us for disturbing the peace."

Her mom chuckled. "He does seem to be getting louder. And tonight your dad and I are going out to dinner with Stacy and Max. You're welcome to come along. We'll probably be leaving around seven."

Maddy shook her head. "Sorry, Mom, but I already have a date with Jordan, remember?"

"That's right. If you have a change in plans, you can still come with us."

"Thanks, Mom," said Maddy. She turned and headed toward the sound of the barking and whining. As soon as she stepped into the sunroom, the dog instantly quieted.

Maddy grabbed the television remote and sank down on the couch, thankful for a moment of rest. She flipped the television to a news station and stretched out on the couch. The puppy sat right in front of the television, but Maddy didn't move him because he was too short to block her view. After a few minutes of stock quotes, the puppy was fast asleep, and Maddy felt herself drifting off to sleep. Just as she closed her eyes, the phone rang. Maddy sat up, and grabbed the cordless from the coffee table.

"Hello?"

"Hello? Could I speak with Madison Thompson, please?" the woman on the other end asked.

"This is she."

"Madison, this is Mrs. Calvin at the Mevlom Institute. I just wanted to let you know that you got the job."

"Great! When do I start?"

"The camp doesn't start for two more weeks, but we have faculty orientation next week, starting Monday. We'll spend most of the time going over the curriculum so the teachers can get their lesson plans together. Just show up at the institute on Monday at nine, and we'll go from there."

"Thanks so much."

"We're glad to have you aboard. You have your work cut out for you." She laughed.

"I'm looking forward to it."

"Well, if you don't have any more questions, I'd better get to the rest of my calls."

"No, I'm fine for now. If I need to reach you before Monday. . ."

"Just give me a call here at the institute. If not, I'll see you Monday morning."

"All right." Maddy hung up the phone and reached down to pet the puppy, who had been awakened by the ringing of the phone. "You can go back to sleep now," she told him. Maddy yawned and stretched out again, then fell asleep.

An hour later, Maddy awoke to the sound of a ringing phone. Groggily, she opened her eyes and reached for the receiver. "Hello?"

"Maddy? This is Jordan."

"Oh." Maddy sat up, fully awake. "Hi. You'll never guess who I've been baby-sitting all afternoon."

"I give up," he said.

"Your puppy," Maddy answered. "And, by the way, you never told me his name."

"Oh, I'm sorry about that. Actually, he doesn't have a name yet."

"Oh, really?"

"Yeah, I've been trying to think of one, but nothing sounds good yet. No pets are allowed in my apartment, so my parents are keeping him until I can move somewhere else."

"Well, unfortunately for Mrs. Myston, your parents weren't home today. When I got home a few hours ago, she was planning to stay outside until someone came to get him, because she thought he would wreck her garden. I didn't think she should be out in the heat that long, so I took him for a while."

Jordan sighed. "I'm really sorry to put you through all of this, but I'll take him to my parents' when I come tonight."

"That's fine with me. He hasn't been too much trouble so far. By the way, how should I dress for tonight?"

"That's the reason I was calling. I was having trouble thinking up something really fun to do, so I thought for tonight we could cook for ourselves and just talk for a while."

Maddy felt her heart rate pick up suddenly, and she put her hand on her chest as if she would be able to still the thumping in her chest. "Cook?" she asked.

"Yeah. How about it? I'll bring the food and you supply the kitchen?"

Maddy considered what she should say. On the one hand, she didn't want to put his idea down, especially since he *had* said 'for tonight.' That implied that he might want to get together again, so she didn't want to offend him and ruin any chance she had of seeing him again. On the other hand, she didn't want to relive her home ec days, either. They'd taken the class the same semester and he had used her kitchen mishaps as the topic of many jokes. Was he trying to embarrass her again, even after his big apology? Maddy shrugged. She might as well be up front with him, and see what he would say.

"Actually, I'm not so sure about that, Jordan. I can't believe you've forgotten how bad I was in home ec. I don't think I've really progressed too far beyond that stage, so I don't think I would be much help to you, as far as dinner goes."

Jordan laughed heartily. "Oh, come on, Maddy. Everybody learns how to cook in college, if only of necessity. You can't be as bad as you were back then."

"I'm serious," Maddy said.

"I'm sure you're joking, but if it makes you feel any better, I'll do most of the cooking. I'll be the head chef and you can be my assistant. Is that better?"

"Okay. . . ," she relented. "But I'm telling you the truth. Just don't be surprised if I can't do too much," she said.

"Okay. Just have the kitchen ready, and I'll do the rest," he said.

"That sounds like a plan. What time should I expect you?"

"I'd say around six-thirty or so. We should be eating by eight, at the latest."

"Do you know what we're going to be cooking?" she asked.

"Not really. I'll just have to see what grabs my attention at the market," he said. "And will your parents be eating with us?"

"I don't think so," she said. "They're going out for dinner with my sister and her husband."

"Then I'll see you in a couple hours," he said before hanging up.

Maddy hung up the phone and tried to calm the nervousness that was rising in the pit of her stomach. "What have I gotten myself into?" she asked the puppy. He just wagged his tail and licked her toes. She sighed and reached down to pet his fluffy head. "Stacy was right," she told him. "I don't know the first thing about cooking, and Jordan's not going to be too impressed with that. Stay here and be quiet," she told the puppy. He seemed to understand, and stretched out on the floor as if he were about to take another nap.

Maddy headed upstairs to ask her mother for advice. This time, she found Berniece curled up in an overstuffed armchair reading a book.

"Mom?" said Maddy.

"Yes?" Berniece closed the book and looked at Maddy expectantly.

"I have a slight change of plans. Jordan's coming over tonight. He wants to cook."

Berniece nodded. "That's fine."

Maddy sat down on the floor next to the chair. "He wants me to *help* him cook. I don't cook."

"Just tell him you're a little rusty in that area. I'm sure he'll understand."

Maddy shook her head. "I tried, but he thinks that I'm exaggerating."

"Well, in that case, I think you're going to have to tough it out. Cooking's not that hard, as long as you follow the directions, you know." Berniece smiled. "And I don't think it's a really big deal. If you have a question, just ask him. I'm sure he's no gourmet chef. Just stick with the recipe and you'll be fine."

Maddy groaned in frustration. "I have a bad feeling about this."

Berniece laughed. "Just be honest and don't worry about it." She glanced at her watch and stood up. "It's almost four-thirty and I need to decide what I'm wearing tonight. And after all that painting today, I think my fingernails could use a coat of polish." She looked down at Maddy, who still sat on the floor. "Don't get too upset about it, sweetie. If he really likes you, he's not going to care about you not learning how to cook. And if it still bothers you, it's never too late to learn. Think about it. With your computer work, you have to follow a lot of directions. Cooking's not that much different." Then she turned and headed to her bedroom.

Maddy stayed seated on the floor. *Maybe Mom is right. It's not too late for me to learn.* Feeling the effects of her new-found determination, she stood up and headed to her room to fix her hair and get dressed. While she waited for Jordan, she would look over her mother's cookbooks. *I'll try to at least familiarize myself with some cooking jargon.*

five

Almost two hours later, Maddy was surrounded by cook-books in the kitchen, when she heard the garage door open, signaling that her dad had gotten home from work. When he entered the kitchen, his eyes widened.

"Don't make any jokes, Dad," she warned playfully.

"Okay, I won't. But what's with all the cookbooks? Didn't Mom tell you that we're going out for dinner tonight?"

"You and Mom are, but I'm staying here because Jordan is coming over and I'm helping him cook dinner tonight."

Her dad arched an eyebrow and said, "Jordan?"

"Yes, Jordan."

"When is he coming?"

"He should be here in a few minutes."

Her dad laughed. "And you're trying to take a speed course in cooking before he gets here?"

Maddy shrugged. "Kind of, but it's pretty hard. I don't know if any of it is really sinking in." Before she could say more, the doorbell rang. "That's him," said Maddy. She quickly began putting the cookbooks back on the shelves.

"I'll get the door," said her dad. "Do you want me to stall him while you hide your textbooks?"

Maddy playfully rolled her eyes. "No, thanks, I'll be fin-ished by the time he gets in here."

Her dad laughed even harder this time as he left to answer the door. "Even so, I'll walk really slowly," he called back to her.

Maddy finished putting the books up and looked over the kitchen. At least it was clean. *I might not be the greatest cook, but at least I know how to clean a kitchen.* She rested her hands on the island and tried to look casual as she waited for her dad to come back with Jordan. *Lord, please let him be planning to cook something relatively simple. . .like spaghetti,* she prayed.

The two men entered the room, each carrying a brown paper bag of groceries.

"Hey, Maddy," said Jordan. Looking around the kitchen, he remarked, "I guess you're ready to get started."

"Ready as I'll ever be," she said, forcing herself to smile. Meanwhile, her stomach flipped while she wondered what type of cooking duty she would be given.

"I guess I'll let you two get started. I don't want to hold up the meal," said her dad as he set the bag on the island. He waved good-bye and left Maddy and Jordan in the kitchen.

Jordan set his bag down, also. "When I pulled up, I saw the lights on at my parents' so I guess I'll take the puppy over there before we get started. Could you show me where he is?"

Maddy pointed to the sunroom. "He's out there. The door in there leads to the backyard."

"Thanks." Jordan walked toward the sunroom.

"Oh—what about the food? Should I put it somewhere? Like the cabinets or refrigerator?" Maddy asked him.

Jordan shrugged. "You can lay everything out, but I don't think you need to refrigerate anything, except the fruit and the yogurt, unless you really want to. We'll just pull it all back out, since we're about to get started."

"Oh," she said, feeling a little silly. "Right. I'll just lay everything out."

As soon as he left the room, Maddy began emptying the bags. First, she pulled out a couple tomatoes. *Good. Tomatoes are in spaghetti. Maybe I can pull this off after all.* Then she pulled out vinegar, olive oil, and a can of sun-dried tomatoes. Next, she found a can of artichokes, a jar of red peppers, cherry tomatoes, green onions, and garlic. *What's with all the tomatoes?* She was starting to worry. She'd emptied one bag and so far, she hadn't seen any pasta or tomato sauce. Maybe it wasn't spaghetti after all.

She moved on to the next bag. There she found cherry juice, strawberries, raspberries, mozzarella cheese, vanilla yogurt, cranberry juice, a lemon, a loaf of sourdough bread, and cheese tortellini. Maddy suddenly felt tired. This was obviously beyond spaghetti. *How am I going to keep up?* She rubbed her aching temples.

Jordan came back through the door, carrying several assorted cuttings of green plants. He grinned. "Let's get started, because I'm starving." He handed Maddy the plants and said, "I guess you'll need to rinse them off. I just pulled them from my mom's garden." Looking around, he said, "I'll need a few pots and pans."

Maddy pointed to the cabinet where her mom kept all the cookware. While Jordan was busy getting a pot of water to boil, Maddy puzzled over the plants she was holding. *What an odd gift,* she thought. Never could she remember having received a bouquet of plants instead of flowers. But Jordan was not the average guy. He was an artist. . .so maybe he thought plants were nicer than flowers. *Still, it would have been nice to have a few flowers mixed in with these.* She leaned over to smell them and was pleasantly surprised. They were highly fragrant, and almost smelled good enough to eat.

Smiling, she went over to the sink and rinsed them off as Jordan had directed. She also couldn't remember having to rinse off a bouquet of flowers. She ran the plants under some cool water and sat them on the counter while she looked for a nice vase to set them in. A few moments later, she found a medium-sized vase and partially filled it with water. She looked in the pantry and found the aspirin her mother kept for flowers and crushed a couple. She added the aspirin to the water and then tried to arrange the plants to look pretty. After she was done, she stood back to admire her work. It was certainly unusual, but it would make a nice centerpiece for the table. She went to put the vase on the dining room table, then returned back to the kitchen where Jordan was busily chopping the onions.

Mustering all of her courage, she asked, "What can I do?"

Jordan looked up from his work and smiled. "Let's see. How are you with vinaigrette?"

"Excuse me?" she asked.

"I need a tomato vinaigrette for this salad," he said.

"Oh. Well, just tell me what I need to do and I'll do my best. By the way, what are we making?"

Jordan laughed. "Sorry about that! I haven't even told you what we're having. For dinner we'll make a tortellini salad with tomato vinaigrette along with bruschetta with roasted peppers and mozzarella. For dessert, I thought we'd have fruit smoothies."

Maddy blinked. She hoped the panic she felt didn't show on her face. How in the world was she supposed to make a vinaigrette? "Wow. That sounds like something we'd have at a restaurant. I didn't know you were such a good cook."

"Well, I went to cooking school for two semesters in New York," he said. "And I also worked at a restaurant for a little while. So I can't say it came naturally."

"Now about this vinaigrette. . ." Maddy managed what she hoped was a lighthearted chuckle. "It's been a while since I've made one, so you'll need to refresh my memory," she fibbed.

He handed her a grater and a bowl. "This is a tomato vinaigrette, so you'll need to cut the tomatoes in half and rub them over the grater until there's nothing left but the skin. Then add a little minced garlic, a couple of tablespoons of vinegar and olive oil, and whisk it together. Got it?"

Maddy nodded. "It's all coming back to me now." This she could handle. While she worked, she struck up a conversation. "So what do you do exactly?"

"I paint. Mostly murals." Jordan stirred the tortellini, then resumed slicing the roasted peppers. "Right now, I'm working on three. Two for churches and one residential."

"So you must really enjoy it?" Maddy questioned. She slowly rubbed the tomato back and forth on the grater.

Hopefully, if she went slowly enough, she would be able to do this for the entire time Jordan cooked.

"Oh yeah. I love it. Right now, the ones in the churches are for a nursery and a Sunday school class. It's basically kind of a big Bible picture book theme."

"What about the residential one?"

Jordan sighed. "It's supposed to be a big abstract in really bright colors. The lady is having me paint a whole wall of her living room in neon colors."

Maddy's eyes widened. "Neon?"

"Yeah."

"You don't sound like you're enjoying that one too much."

"I guess I am. The problem is, she wants to tell me how to paint it. I think she would be more satisfied if I handed her the brush and let her do it herself." He laughed.

"How do you find work?"

"Sometimes by word of mouth, especially with the residential projects. Then I do a lot of advertising and handing out business cards wherever I go."

"Sounds like fun. So what's your next big project?"

"Actually, my next project is going to be the most exciting one I've done yet. I've been looking for a place to move where I can keep my dog, which was why I hadn't been able to get back over here sooner."

Maddy nodded. "Did you find a place?"

He grinned. "Actually, I was more successful than I'd expected to be. I'm trying to decide between three places."

"Are any of them near here?" she asked.

He shook his head. "No. I wouldn't be able to find what I want in south Kansas City. I've been looking downtown, near the City Market."

Maddy raised her eyebrows. "The City Market? What are you looking for? An old warehouse?"

Jordan's eyes lit up. "Pretty close. I've narrowed my choices down to three loft spaces downtown."

"Really?" she asked. "That's pretty interesting. For a long

time, I didn't even know we had loft space in Kansas City. It seems so. . .New York, or something."

"I know. I rented a loft when I lived there, but I didn't do too much to it in the decorating sense. But now that I'm getting settled here, I wanted to take a huge open area and really take the time to decorate it the way I want. So I've spent the last two or three weeks checking out different spaces, and I think I'm pretty close to making a decision. I'll probably move within the next month or two."

"That's pretty soon. Are you all packed?"

He laughed. "Not really. But I don't really have too much stuff. I could move with one truckload. I've been holding off buying a lot of furniture until I could find a more permanent place. And now, it looks like I'm almost there."

"Well, I've never been inside a loft, so once you get settled, you'll have to let me come over and take a look," she told him.

"I will," he said.

Her parents entered the kitchen. "Hi, Jordan," said her mother.

"Hello, Mrs. Thompson," he replied.

"Everything smells delicious. I hate to miss out on this," said her dad.

"We'll save you a taste," Jordan promised.

"We're headed over to meet Max and Stacy," said her mother. "We have the cell phone, so call if you need us."

"Okay," replied Maddy. Her parents glanced at her bowl of tomatoes with raised eyebrows, but didn't comment before they left.

She and Jordan worked in silence for the next few minutes, until Jordan spoke up. "How's the vinaigrette coming?" he asked her.

"It's coming," she said brightly.

He turned to the stove, lifted the pot of tortellini and carried it to the sink where he drained it, then rinsed it under running water.

Maddy completed her grated tomatoes. She couldn't

remember how much oil and vinegar she was supposed to add, and Jordan was busy mixing the tortellini with the other ingredients he'd chopped, so she just guessed.

She remembered that Jordan hadn't used any measuring spoons or cups, so she decided to try to eyeball the measurements like he had done. She lifted the bottle of olive oil and poured a steady stream of it for about ten seconds. She stirred it, but it looked a little too thick to her. In addition, the oil kept separating from the tomatoes. When she added the vinegar, she put in twice as much vinegar as the oil, hoping to thin the mixture out a little. What resulted was a pink, blotchy mess that wouldn't blend together. In addition, the vinegar smell was really strong. She stirred vigorously, trying to make the oil blend in better.

A few moments later, Jordan looked up. "What's that smell?" he asked, his nose twitching.

Maddy's cheeks started to burn. She decided to act like she didn't understand what he was talking about. "I don't smell anything." She pointed to the area where he was working. "It might be the onions."

He sniffed. "No, it smells like vinegar," he said, looking toward her mixing bowl.

"Oh, that." Maddy swallowed. She covered the bowl slightly and turned away. "I just added the vinegar to my sauce."

"How much?" he said.

Maddy was at a loss for words. "Why don't you work on your dish and I'll work on mine." She abruptly turned and headed to the walk-in pantry, taking her bowl with her. In answer to his raised eyebrows, she said, "I need to add some of my special vinaigrette ingredients."

Once she was safely inside the pantry, she tried to decide what to do. Obviously, the vinegar was too strong. Should she add more tomatoes or try to tone down the vinegar some other way? She looked around frantically. *Maybe more olive oil,* she thought. She shook her head and tried to think what her mom would do if this happened. As she scanned the shelves, she had a dim memory of someone saying to put a potato in something if it got too salty. She found a potato and left the bowl in the pantry while she went back in the kitchen to rinse and slice it.

Quickly, she rinsed, sliced and chopped the potato, then added it to the mixture, wondering how long it would take to absorb the extra vinegar. She dipped a finger in the mixture and tasted it. It was so sour it burned her tongue. Making a face, she realized the potato was not going to be enough. As she scanned the shelves again, her eyes rested on a bag of sugar. *That should do the trick.* She quickly poured a generous amount of sugar into the bowl and stirred it. Now it was a grainy, pink liquid with big chunks of potato that still smelled like vinegar.

Maddy frowned. Even if the sugar cut the vinegary taste, Jordan would probably realize that it was too pink. She'd had tomato vinaigrette before and it was much redder. She looked around until she found a box containing small boxes of food coloring. One held a green liquid, another held blue, and two held a red liquid. Maddy grabbed one and poured in a fair amount of the reddish liquid. When she stirred it, it turned pinkish orange. "What in the world?" She looked at the bottles again, and realized she'd used the *yellow* dye instead of the red.

"Oh, great," she said. Then Jordan knocked on the door. "Maddy? Are you okay in there?"

"Um, yeah. I'm coming right out." Maddy opened the door and came out without her bowl.

"Where's the vinaigrette?" he asked. "I'm almost ready to put it on the salad."

"I'm leaving it in there for a few minutes. To let it sort of. . . mesh," she told him. "Is there anything else I can do?"

"You could work on the bruschetta. I've already made a spread, so you just slice the bread, put the spread on it, add a little mozzarella, and put it in the oven."

"I'll start on that now," she said.

"Oh, and Maddy, where are the herbs?"

"The what?"

"The herbs. You know, the basil, oregano, rosemary. . ." He looked at her expectantly.

"Oh. They're in the pantry. I'll bring them right out. You just stay right here." Maddy rushed to the pantry and quickly gathered several bottles of dried herbs. "Here they are," she said when she returned to the kitchen.

"Not these," he said.

"Not these?" she repeated.

He shook his head. "I was talking about the fresh ones I brought."

She looked at him blankly. "I don't know what you're talking about."

He laughed. "C'mon, Maddy. Don't joke with me. Remember, I brought over some fresh herbs from my mom's garden. I handed them to you."

Maddy gasped. "Oh *those* herbs."

He nodded, grinning. "Yeah, those. Where are they?"

Maddy wanted to melt into the floor. So far, she'd ruined a vinaigrette and mistaken fresh herbs for a bouquet of greenery. She pointed toward the dining room. "They're in there," she said quietly. "On the table."

While Jordan went to get the plants, Maddy wondered how she would explain why she'd arranged fresh herbs in a vase.

Jordan came back a few seconds later with a grin on his face. "I got the herbs. And I must say, it's too bad we have to eat them, because they look so pretty like this," he said. "Can you tell me what this white stuff in the water is?"

Maddy wordlessly turned and went into the pantry. She grabbed the bowl of what had started out as vinaigrette and showed it to Jordan. "Okay. I have a confession. I've never made a vinaigrette. In fact, I can't cook. The only work I ever do in a kitchen is washing dishes."

"And the herbs?" he asked.

Maddy closed her eyes. "I thought they were a gift for me. Like flowers, except without. . .any flowers. So I put some aspirin in the water to help keep them alive. I didn't realize what they were."

Jordan appeared to be trying to refrain from laughing for a few seconds. Then he finally said something. "Don't feel bad. Anyone can make a mistake," he told her.

"You're not going to tease me about this?" she asked.

"Not the way I would have in high school. I can't promise you I won't crack a few smiles over it. I can't even promise that I'll never mention it again, but I won't do it in a mean way."

"Okay," said Maddy. "What do we do about the vinaigrette?"

"It looks like I'll start over. And you can just. . .watch." He leaned over and stirred the mixture in the bowl. "I'm not even going to ask what's in there."

"Good. Because I wouldn't tell you anyway," she said firmly.

"Listen, I'm going to run over to my parents' and grab some more herbs. You just wait here, okay?"

"Okay." Maddy sat down on one of the stools that her mom kept at the counter, while Jordan opened the door.

"Don't cook anything while I'm gone," he called over his shoulder.

❧

Jordan chuckled as he snipped herbs for the second time that evening. Maddy had been so cute, trying to impress him with her cooking skills. He was just glad she hadn't tried to act like nothing was wrong and asked him to eat it, because he didn't think he would have been able to swallow it.

He had figured something was going wrong when he had started smelling the excess vinegar that she had very liberally poured into the bowl, but he didn't know what she could have done to it while she was in the pantry. By the time she shut herself in the small room and then tried to slip out to rinse off a potato, he'd had to bite his tongue to keep from making a joke that might have hurt her feelings.

He had to walk a fine line in his newly cultivated friendship with Maddy for two reasons. Even though most of his friends knew him as a really easygoing guy with a penchant for humor, he still had trouble deciding what type of jokes were funny and what cracks were mean. When he was younger, it hadn't mattered—he had just wanted to get a laugh. But now that he was a Christian, he was keenly aware of the fact that at the end of his life, he would have to answer to the Lord for everything he had done, thought, and spoken. And he didn't want to stand at the door to Heaven trying to explain away some of the harsher humor he had let slip out. Secondly, with Maddy, the last thing he wanted to do was verbally tear her down. If anything, he wanted to build her up, to help her see how special she was. She seemed unsure of herself sometimes, and he wondered if any of his teasing in high school had an effect on how she viewed herself.

Too many times he saw someone he had gone to high school with, and during the conversation, the person would tense up, trying to brace himself for more teasing. Five years ago he might have said, "It's just a joke. Lighten up a little." But he'd experienced an event that had taught him what kind of damage verbal abuse could do. And it didn't have to be done in a mean-spirited way. Jokes could scar a person's soul just as badly as a loud, angry tirade spewn forth by an abusive bully.

Harper Blackston. The name came to his mind out of nowhere. . .and everywhere. Reflexively, Jordan squeezed his hands into fists, his fingernails digging into the flesh of his palms. The name was one he'd tried to erase from his memory, and yet it somehow had seared itself into everything that he did. He couldn't forget it. He couldn't hide it. He couldn't escape it. Jordan stood up so fast that he felt dizzy for a second. He put his hand on his forehead and wiped away beads of sweat.

"Therefore, there is now no condemnation for those who are in Christ Jesus," he whispered. Romans 8:1 had been the first Bible verse he had learned, and the one that he now leaned on the most.

The man who led him to Christ had shown him that verse, and Jordan prayed the prayer of salvation because he liked the hope the verse offered. In fact, it had been one of the main reasons he had accepted Christ. He hadn't become a Christian simply to gain entrance into Heaven after he died, or even to be able to worship at Christ's throne for all eternity, because those things had not even entered his mind at the time.

Instead he had taken hold of salvation because he had experienced a fleeting moment of reality. Frankly, he had had to admit to himself that he knew very little when it came to matters of eternity, and he'd been scared. But Jordan had been in awe of the fact that God wanted to grant man forgiveness so much that He let His only Son be the sacrifice for all of man's sins, both reckless and premeditated. Since the forgiveness was his for the asking, Jordan had eagerly asked and received.

Almost ironically, his faith in the truth of that verse was put to the test. And for a long time, his faith failed. During that period, Romans 8:1 alone hadn't seemed enough. And he'd nearly drowned while being tossed in the sea of horror his conscience had created for him. Then, when he'd given up almost any hope, an unexpected ally had tossed him a lifeline, leading him back to Romans 8, in addition to Isaiah 43:25, which had comforted him almost instantly. At first, it had been almost unfathomable to imagine that God would blot out his sins and not even remember them. But he'd finally accepted and believed it.

Yet, even today, nearly three years later, he was keenly aware of another fact. While God might wash his sins as white as snow, Jordan could still remember them. Unless someone came up with a pill to make the mind successfully dislodge unwanted memories, he was stuck with the memory of the part he'd played in the whole ordeal.

He would never forget. And it haunted him. . .teased him. Worse yet, he couldn't talk to anyone about it. His parents didn't want to hear it anymore. The people at his church might react any number of ways, and Jordan didn't want to take the risk of finding out what they would say. And Maddy—he couldn't risk destroying their friendship so soon by telling her. It was his own solitary burden to bear. It was between him, God, and Harper Blackston, who would never speak to a living soul again.

"Jordan?" Maddy's voice drifted to him over the fence. "Where are you?"

He looked around to see her standing on the deck of her house. "Over here," he said as he made his way back to her yard. The sunset was in the beginning stages and the warm glow of the sun spilled across the yard, enveloping them in elegant gold sprinkles.

His heart caught in his throat for a moment as he stared at Maddy. She was smiling at him, and he couldn't recall ever seeing her smile like that. She smiled at him as though he had never said a mean word to her. Just like that, she had forgiven him, and he found it hard to believe. With God, he could understand, but he never really believed that another human being would be able to offer forgiveness so freely. He had apologized to others just as sincerely as he had to Maddy, but they hadn't responded with the same warmth Maddy had extended. She was beautiful, and he couldn't deny that he felt a stirring in his heart when he thought of her. But even if she weren't in another relationship, he didn't think she would let herself ever develop romantic feelings for him again, and even if she did. . .she wouldn't want to be involved with him if she knew what he had done.

Still, he couldn't restrain himself from breaking off a small branch from his mother's lilac tree. When he reached Maddy's porch, he presented her with the lilacs.

"Thanks," she said, leaning over to sniff the light purple blossoms. "You really didn't have to."

"I did it because I wanted to," he said in a really bad imitation of a southern accent. He deepened his voice a notch and said, "It was unchivalrous of me not to bring you flowers tonight in the first place."

Maddy laughed and batted her eyelashes. In a high pitched southern accent that was only slightly better than his, she said, "Then I'll just add these to the fragrant greenery you gave me earlier." As she turned to head inside, he grabbed her hand and pulled her back.

In response to the questioning look on her face, he said softly, "You have something on your cheek." He lifted his hand to her face and brushed away a small tomato seed that had glued itself to her face. He marveled at the softness of her cheek and left his hand on her face a second longer than was necessary. As he considered kissing her, she closed her eyes and leaned toward him slightly.

Jordan sighed and removed his hand from her cheek. She had looked at him with such trust that it nearly broke his heart. He was going to have to put a stop to things before they got started. He cleared his throat. "I guess we should go ahead and finish up so we can eat. I'll do the vinaigrette, and you can do the bruschetta, okay?" With that, he opened the door and strode into the house, and Maddy wordlessly followed.

❧

Maddy could have cried, but she didn't. If she wasn't mistaken, Jordan had been about two seconds away from kissing her, but had apparently changed his mind. *What did I do?* she wondered as she spread Jordan's roasted pepper paste on the slices of bread she had cut.

Since they had come back in the kitchen, he had barely even looked at her again. *Am I that unattractive? "Maddy the mutant."* Maddy blinked in surprise as she remembered the familiar chant. A visual memory of Jordan laughing and teasing her sprang up in her mind's eye. Was that how he really felt about her? Was she imagining the almost kiss, or had he planned it that way? Did he feel attracted to her even a little or was this some sort of elaborate joke?

She finished putting the mozzarella on the bread and put the baking sheet in the oven. When she finished, she turned around and caught Jordan staring at her. She smiled at him and he gave her a stiff grin in return, then busied himself with the tortellini salad. *Lord, what's going on here?* she prayed. *Am I doing something wrong, or does he like me and he just feels unsure of what to do?*

At any rate, she was determined to make the evening less uncomfortable for both of them, so she decided to strike up a conversation. "So tell me more about your puppy," she said brightly.

Jordan looked relieved and said, "There's not too much to tell. He doesn't have a name yet because I can't think of one. He's two months old, and he manages to escape from my parents' yard every day, wreaking all manner of havoc in all of our neighbors' yards, yet he doesn't touch a single plant in my mother's garden. How's that for an interesting pet?"

Maddy laughed. "I think he's acting out because you're neglecting him. Maybe you should try to spend a little more quality time with the poor thing," she quipped.

Jordan laughed in response. "Maybe you're right. I'll take him to the park next Saturday. I'd take him this Saturday, but I've already planned to work. Why don't you to come with us?"

"Only if I wouldn't be imposing," she replied.

"Of course not," he said. "We'd love to have you come. How about it?"

"I wouldn't miss it," she smiled. She pulled the bread out of the oven and sighed with relief. Everything seemed to be normal again.

six

The next week passed in a blur for Maddy. She spent her days in training sessions for her new job as a computer instructor at the Mevlom day camp, and she spent her evenings settling back into her parents' home. She unpacked all of her boxes from school and found that she had accumulated quite a collection of things in her dorm room. So much, in fact, that her room at home wasn't big enough to hold all of her mementos and belongings from both her elementary through high school years and college.

In the evenings she sorted everything out, deciding what to keep, what to throw out, and what to store. The items she threw out were few and far between. She ended up cramming the room as full as she comfortably could, and boxed up the rest, claiming to her protesting parents that she was "storing it all in the attic for a little while until I can think of what to do with it all."

In the back of her mind, she had a feeling that she would probably never throw away any of it, and when the time came for her to move out on her own, she'd probably end up carrying all that stuff with her wherever she went. But she didn't mind. It was part of her history, and that type of thing had always been important to her.

The highlights of that week were the few evenings when Jordan stopped to see her. One night they went to get ice cream, and the next evening they took his puppy for a walk around the neighborhood. That evening, Maddy had just gotten home from work, and when she stepped out of the car, the puppy jumped up and placed his muddy paws on her crème-colored slacks. She'd become furious and fussed at the puppy for a few minutes, and Jordan had offered to pay the cleaning bill. By then, Maddy had softened a little, and she jokingly suggested that he name the puppy "Muddy," since he was covered in mud most of the time.

Jordan thought it was a good choice, but joked that he didn't want to name the dog "Muddy," because it started with the same letter as Maddy's name, and sooner or later, he would probably start mixing them up. So he decided to name the dog John Hancock, and Hancock for short, in keeping with the same general idea of how the puppy was always leaving his signature, or "John Hancock" on people's legs.

Friday evening, she had reluctantly gone to play laser tag with the singles' group at her church. She had really wanted to stick around the house and see if Jordan might stop by, but her best friend Laina had insisted Maddy come along. The two of them had been best friends since they met at vacation Bible school in the second grade. Although Laina had gone to college in Kansas City, and Maddy had chosen Texas Southern, they had kept in touch and had remained close.

Maddy had been neglecting Laina in favor of Jordan since their first date, and Laina made her feel more than a little guilty for it. "I don't know what's going on with you, but I get the feeling you're trying to avoid me," she had gently teased. "But if you don't come tonight, I'll come over there myself and find out what's going on." She laughed.

"Okay, okay, I'll go," Maddy conceded. Laina had been there for her during her ill-fated crush on Jordan in high school, and the last thing she wanted was Laina to come over while she and Jordan were visiting. Maddy had been pretty quick to forgive him, but her best friend knew how much he had hurt her. Knowing Laina, she wouldn't be so trusting of Jordan's apology.

So she went with Laina and had a good time, while opting not to mention Jordan just yet. Her parents had also been gone for the evening, so Maddy had no way of knowing if Jordan had stopped by.

When Maddy awoke on Saturday, she spent most of the

morning in a flurry of excitement in anticipation of spending the afternoon at the park with Jordan and Hancock.

When Jordan pulled up to the curb that afternoon, Maddy went outside to meet him, and a few moments later, Hancock came trotting up the street, his paws covered in his favorite medium.

"He's been at it again," said Maddy.

"Oh, no," Jordan groaned. "What have you gotten into today?" Jordan asked the puppy, who jumped up and planted his paws on his legs.

"I don't know," answered Maddy, "But if we wait a couple of minutes, I'm sure one of the neighbors will probably come over and let us know."

"I guess they can tell my parents the extent of the damage," said Jordan. "So let's go to the park."

They decided to go to Jacob Loose Park, which had a small lake and a big area where Hancock would be able to run around.

When they got there, Maddy was surprised that Jordan had packed a small lunch. "I could've put something together, if you had asked me," she remarked as he began pulling items from a picnic basket.

"Well—" He looked at her uncertainly. "It wasn't too much trouble, and I figured you were probably too tired from your first week at work to go through any extra trouble."

Maddy stopped pouring the glasses of lemonade and stared at him for a moment. "Translation," she said sarcastically, "is that you don't think I'm a good enough cook to be entrusted with making lunch."

Jordan wiggled his eyebrows. "No comment there. Now, are you ready to eat?" He held up two bags of potato chips. "I got regular and salt and *vinegar*. . .in your honor."

Maddy arched her eyebrows. "Ha, ha, ha, *so* funny." Taking the lid off of a container, she said, "This smells really good."

Jordan shrugged. "It's just grilled cheese. And it's not even hot anymore."

"It smells delicious." Maddy took a bite and found it tasted even better than it smelled. "Umm. . .I like it. And it's not your run-of-the-mill grilled cheese. What's in it?"

Jordan turned to Hancock, who was edging closer and closer to the blanket and the food. "Sit still, boy. I've got a treat for you." He opened up a bag of doggie treats and tossed a few to the puppy. Then he answered Maddy's question. "Smoked Gouda on jalapeno and sun-dried tomato focaccia."

"I assume you baked the bread yourself."

"No," said Jordan. After a short pause he added, "I've been too busy to bake this week."

Maddy playfully tossed a chip at him. "My goodness, aren't you feeling a little conceited today?"

"Hey, a man shouldn't be ashamed if he's got skills in the kitchen, right?"

"I guess not. I just wish I had a little more culinary knowledge," she grumbled.

"Don't worry about it, okay? Some people have it and some. . .don't." Jordan rubbed his hand across his smooth scalp and grinned.

Maddy rolled her eyes. "Oh, goodness." She laughed.

For a few minutes, neither of them spoke. Jordan finished his sandwich, wiped his hands on a napkin, then asked, "I came over to see you last night, but nobody was home. You and your parents go out to dinner or something?"

Maddy shook her head. "My best friend Laina was after me to hang out with her, so we went to play laser tag with the singles' group at our church."

He nodded, wordlessly.

"I would have invited you if you had come over sooner."

Jordan waved his hands. "Nah, I wouldn't want to come barging in on you and your group."

Maddy laughed. "Oh, come on. You wouldn't be barging in. You would be my guest."

"That's really okay," he said firmly. "Besides, I hang out with the singles' class at my church sometimes, too."

Is he trying to give me a hint or something? Maddy wondered. Shyly, she asked, "Are you seeing someone at your church?"

"Me? Nah. Why else would I be spending so much time with you?"

"You said we were seeing each other just as friends," reminded Maddy. "I distinctly remember you telling me you only wanted to be friends." *Is he getting ready to ask me out on a more serious basis?* she wondered.

"Yeah. . .I haven't forgotten about that," he said slowly.

Maddy's heart dropped. *What kind of game is he playing?* Her mind raced back to their dinner together last week. Out on the deck, she was certain he had wanted to kiss her, and then his demeanor had totally changed. And now, he had almost acted a little jealous of her going out with her church group, and then he had admitted he only wanted to be friends. From now on, she wasn't going to make herself so vulnerable to him. If he wanted to know how she felt about him, he'd have to be a little more honest about his own feelings.

Reaching over to pet Hancock, who was starting to whimper, Maddy said, "Why don't we go for a walk? He's been pretty good to sit here while we ate."

Jordan held up the empty bag of doggie treats. "Are you kidding? It took these to keep him from snatching our lunch off our plates." He stood up and stretched, and Maddy tried not to stare at his long, muscular arms.

She stood up and folded the blanket and handed it to Jordan, who went to put it in his car along with the basket before they took a walk around the park.

When he returned, Maddy was busy trying to keep Hancock from jumping up on her.

"Hancock! Sit!" ordered Jordan. The puppy grew still and sat down. Jordan held up a leash in his hand. "I probably should have put this on him a few weeks ago. But I think now's probably a good time to start," he said. They spent the next few minutes trying to keep the wriggling puppy still long enough to fasten the leash to his collar.

Finally, they began their journey around the park. After a rough start, Hancock got used to the leash and happily strayed as far as the long cord would let him. Whenever they got close to another group of people, Jordan would gently shorten the leash, giving himself a little more control of the puppy's wanderings.

As they drew closer to the park's famous rose garden, Jordan suddenly asked, "So what about you? Are you seeing somebody?"

Maddy looked at him out of the corner of her eye. *Not even twenty minutes later, he's at it again,* she thought wryly. *This time, I'm not going to be so transparent.* She shook her head and shrugged. "No," was her simple answer.

"Oh, really?"

"Really," she nodded.

"Not even someone at your church?" he questioned.

Maddy tried not to smile. *So that was why he kept asking about where she'd been last night.* "No one," she said. *If that doesn't answer his question, I don't know what will.*

Jordan furrowed his brow. "So who all was there last night?"

"Why in the world are you asking me all of these questions?" Maddy wanted to know. "It was just a bunch of friends from church. You probably wouldn't know them."

Jordan shrugged. "Try me. So who was there?"

Maddy rolled her eyes. "Let's see, my best friend Laina, Gabriella, Vincent, Luke, Tisha, Rakim, Autumn, and Tiffanee. Do you know any of them?"

Jordan frowned. "I kind of remember your friend Laina. Didn't she go to high school with us?"

"Yeah," Maddy nodded. It was a nice feeling to hear Jordan refer to the two of them as 'us.'

"Was anybody else there?"

Maddy groaned. "Wow, you sure are being thorough all of a sudden. JaShandra, and Cole. . .and Arnold, of course."

Arnold Jenkins and his wife, Patty had been in charge of the youth group for as long as she could remember, and they had recently decided to start up a singles' group as well. Unfortunately, Patty hadn't been able to make it last night, because she had twisted her ankle during an aerobics class. Maddy smiled, thinking of how miserable Arnold had looked last night. Laser tag was obviously not his idea of a good time. For a couple in their sixties, Patty and Arnold tried to plan activities that appealed to the young members of the group.

"Oh, really?" said Jordan. "So you were holding out on me the first time?"

Maddy giggled. "Okay, so sue me. I forgot a couple of names."

"Some important names, I might add," said Jordan. His jawline grew firm and he was quiet.

"What are you talking about?" Maddy was bewildered.

"You didn't mention Arnold the first time around," he said tersely. "I would consider him an important name."

Maddy tried to figure out what was going on. "Okay. . . yeah, I guess you could say Arnold's pretty important to the group."

"And to you? What do you think about him?"

"Huh?" Maddy was puzzled. She figured she must've told him about Arnold and Patty starting the group, but she couldn't figure out why he was making such a case out of it.

"Would you be there if Arnold wasn't there?" he continued.

Maddy shrugged. "I guess not," she admitted. "I mean, it was basically his idea to get together and everything. He's the one who keeps the group together."

"So what do you and Arnold talk about?"

Maddy chuckled. "What, are you kidding? I've known Arnold for almost as long as I can remember, but we don't exactly have really long chats. He might call occasionally to let me know if something's going on, but other than that. . . " She shrugged, not knowing what to say. "He's way too busy to sit down and just talk to me for no reason," she finished lamely. "Besides, he usually has Patty to talk to."

They had now reached the outer edges of the rose garden and Maddy heard the familiar strains of "Pachelbel's Canon in D." It sounded like there was a wedding in the rose garden today. Maddy smiled, remembering some of the pleasant memories she had from working with Stacy and the many weddings she'd helped coordinate last summer. "I think it would be so romantic to get married out here in the rose garden," she told Jordan, hoping to ease some of the tension.

He looked at her, and seemed to soften a little. "Yeah, I guess that's pretty cool. Right now, I bet they're just glad it's not raining."

Maddy lowered her voice because they were getting closer to the ceremony. Small weddings of fifty guests or so were common in the rose garden, and it was also common for people who weren't even guests to stand around and quietly watch the ceremony. In fact, it was expected, due to the fact that both the park and the rose garden were public grounds. "Let's get a little closer," she whispered. "I want to see the bride's dress."

Jordan nodded and they reached the outskirts of the pavilion just as the "Wedding March" began. They were as close as they could possibly get without taking a seat next to one of the guests, but they were hidden from sight by several stone pillars that were covered in vines, in addition to a pretty dense covering of assorted rose bushes.

"Where's the music coming from?" Jordan whispered.

"Probably a CD player. There are electrical outlets in some of these pillars. We did that when we did weddings here last summer."

Jordan nodded.

Seconds later, the bride made her entrance. She was beautiful in a long gown with a satin bodice and a wide, fluffy tulle skirt. As Maddy watched the bride make her way down the aisle, she told Jordan, "You might want to shorten Hancock's leash before he walks into the wedding uninvited."

At that moment, the music cut off abruptly. The bride had only made it halfway down the aisle, and she stood there for a moment, confused. There was a general murmur that rippled amongst the gathering of guests, as Maddy realized what was going on. Instantly, she dropped to her knees and began moving among the columns trying to find out where the cord to the CD player needed to be plugged in. Seconds later, she found Hancock tangled up in not only his leash, but also the cord to the CD player. Quickly, Maddy disentangled the cord, and plugged it back in and the "Wedding March" came back on again. Again, Maddy heard a murmuring run through the crowd. *What now?* she thought.

Suddenly, Jordan was kneeling next to her. He quickly unplugged the cord, and when she started to protest, he put his hand over her mouth. "Shhh. Never mind the music," he whispered. "The bride just walked down the aisle in silence and they went ahead and started. When you started the song back up again, they got really confused."

"Oh, sorry," Maddy said sheepishly.

"Let's just get out of here," said Jordan, starting to crawl away.

When they were a safe distance away, they stood up and quickly moved in the other direction.

When they were out of hearing distance, Maddy said, "I can't believe we just messed up a wedding."

Jordan laughed. "I just wish you could've seen the look on the groom's face. I think he might've thought it was a sign or something."

Maddy playfully swatted his arm. "What are you talking about?"

"I've been in a couple of my buddies' weddings, and I was standing there in the bathroom while they lost their lunches five minutes before the ceremony. Believe me, they were having second thoughts. One of them prayed for God to give him a sign if he shouldn't get married." Jordan stopped and bent over from laughing so hard. When he stood up, he finished the story. "What he didn't know was that a friend of ours was hiding in one of the stalls. The guy had been planning some kind of practical joke on me, but when he heard that prayer, he flushed the toilet just to see what we would do."

Maddy put her hands on her hips. "So what happened?"

"Calvin thought God was speaking to him. We didn't know Drew was hiding in there, and we couldn't see his feet, so we figured the toilet was flushing by itself. My buddy jumped up and was about to call the whole thing off until Drew came running out to stop us."

"And did the wedding go on?"

"Yeah. . .after about a thirty-minute delay. The pastor had to pray for him to calm down. That was four years ago. To this day, Calvin's wife still won't let him invite Drew over to the house.

Maddy groaned. "That is so pathetic. I worked at almost thirty weddings last summer, and all of the grooms showed up."

"And you're telling me not one of them got nervous?" Jordan stopped walking and looked at her incredulously.

"Well, all of them had cold feet to a degree, which is understandable, because marriage is a big commitment; but I will add that none of them canceled the wedding."

"Well, it happens," Jordan countered. He started to grin again. "And I know the look. Believe me. . .that man's feet were blocks of ice. If you had messed with that music one more time, he would've bolted." He held his sides from laughing so hard.

"Funny, funny. One day, it'll be your wedding, and you might not have so much to laugh about," she scolded.

Jordan seemed to sober instantly. He cleared his throat. "Nah. . .I'll be fine."

"Is that so?"

"Yeah. I'm not going to ask a woman to marry me unless it's God's will. And if He never gives me the go-ahead, then I'm not going to force it."

Maddy turned and faced him. "Don't you ever want to get married?"

"Yeah. To the right woman. I'm just willing to wait on the

Lord's timing is what I'm trying to say."

"Oh," said Maddy.

"What about you? I noticed you seem to get pretty excited about weddings."

"Of course, I want to get married," she told him.

"But you're not dating anybody," he said. He took hold of her hand and gently held it. "Why not? Hasn't somebody at least caught your eye?"

Maddy didn't know what to say. She didn't really feel comfortable putting her emotions on the line by just telling him that she was interested in him. *Maybe I could just hint, and see if he gets it,* she reasoned. But the problem was how to phrase what she said, without obviously just saying, "I like you." She furrowed her brow and tried to put together a string of sentences to answer his question.

Jordan stopped walking and looked at her carefully. "You still haven't answered my question, you know."

"I know, I just didn't know what to say."

"Just say what you feel."

"Okay." She took a deep breath, and started. "I *am* interested in this guy. I don't really know how he feels about me. Sometimes he's really attentive, and sometimes. . .I don't know. I don't really think I'm his type. And I get the feeling that he might be somewhat interested, but. . ."

"But what?" Jordan wanted to know.

"I'm not really sure. I think he's trying to determine for himself if he could ever be in love with me." There. She'd said it. That practically summed up what she thought about Jordan, and if he couldn't read between the lines, it was his own fault.

"Why not?" he asked. "Why wouldn't he be interested in you?"

Maddy sighed. "I don't know. He's older, and. . .I'm younger. I act a little silly sometimes. I can't cook. I've never kept house." She shrugged in frustration. "I'm just not the 'wifely' type, and I think he's looking for someone who is—

someone who would obviously be a good wife and mother."
Maddy's eyes unexpectedly filled with tears as she put into
words her fears about her budding relationship with Jordan.
She blinked several times and turned away.

Neither of them said anything as they made their way back
to the car. After they rode a few minutes, Jordan spoke again.

"Maddy, those things are not that hard to learn. All you
need is a little practice. And I think you would be a good
wife and mother. Maybe you should just take a chance and
tell him how you feel," he said gently.

Maddy shook her head. Thankfully, Jordan had allowed
her to regain her composure, so she wouldn't have to start
crying in front of him. "I don't think that would be the greatest idea," she told him. "It just wouldn't be practical. We get
along fairly well, so I think it's just best to let things stay the
same and not try to rock the boat."

Jordan shook his head. "I can't say that I agree. Maybe
you should just tell him. You never know what he might say."

"Maybe he should just tell me how he feels about me," she
countered. "Believe me, I've thought about it, and I'm not
going to just tell him."

Jordan's mouth spread into a grin. "There's a verse in the
Bible about that, you know."

"Tell me," Maddy said.

Jordan cleared his throat. "John 8:32. 'Then you will know
the truth, and the truth will set you free.' And it sounds like
you could use a little freedom with this situation. It feels
really good to get things like that out in the open."

Maddy's stomach felt like someone had dropped a rock on
top of it. He was right, but still. . .she couldn't imagine trying
to tell him after this whole conversation that he was the guy
she was talking about. It would be too awkward for both of
them. She turned to face him. "I see your point, but it's not
something I can work up the nerve to do right now."

"Nerves?" Jordan asked.

"Exactly," Maddy answered.

"If you ever need help, you can practice on me," Jordan said helpfully. "That way, you can have a trial run at it. Since I'm your friend, it won't be so uncomfortable."

Maddy stifled a groan. Why on earth would she *practice* telling Jordan to his face that she might be falling in love with him? It was embarrassing to even think about it. "I'll keep that in mind," she said. "But for now, I'd really like to drop this subject." She looked out the window and watched the scenery pass in a blur. It was becoming too unnerving for her to sit here indirectly discussing her feelings for Jordan to his face.

He sighed. "Okay, you know the situation best, so I won't say anything else. But if you ever need to talk to a friend about it, I'm a good listener." He smiled and patted her hand.

A thought popped into her head and before she even seriously considered it, the words came tumbling out of her mouth. "How about helping me learn how to cook?" she asked. Embarrassed, she pursed her lips and started hoping he hadn't heard her.

"What?" He lifted his eyebrows, looking confused.

She sighed. There was no way she could take back what she'd just said. "If you want to be such a good friend, I'm asking you to help me learn how to cook," she repeated.

"I don't mind helping you out, but if you don't mind my asking, how is that going to help the situation?"

She shrugged. "It'd give me a little more confidence to approach him and eventually tell him how I feel about him."

Jordan slowly nodded, his forehead wrinkled. Finally, he spoke. "So you're saying you want me to help you learn how to cook to impress some guy who doesn't know you exist?"

"That's a little harsh, don't you think? He knows I exist. . . he just doesn't know that I like him. And if I told him now, he'd laugh at me. I just need a little time to—"

"Time to make yourself into the kind of woman he thinks you should be," Jordan interrupted her.

"I get the feeling you don't think it's such a good idea,"

Maddy said, not really sure whether or not she should be disappointed. Even she had to admit, it was kind of a silly plan.

Jordan shook his head. "Not really." They turned onto Maddy's street and he slowed the car to a stop in front of her house before he continued. "I mean, what if he decides he likes your cooking, but he decides you would be even more attractive if you were five inches taller and had red hair instead of brown? Would you try to please him then?"

Maddy merely murmured in agreement. In fact, she was kind of glad that the subject hadn't gone much further. It was best to let it drop and move on. If things between her and Jordan were going to get more serious, it would have to happen on its own.

"But I guess I could lend a hand, if you really wanted me to. I did say I would help you out, if you needed me to." Jordan's voice broke into her thoughts. "Soooo. . .when do you want to get started?"

She stared at him, blinking several times while she thought of something to say. *Now what should I do?* she wondered. It wasn't actually a bad plan, once she really thought about it. And if nothing else, it would give her more time with Jordan. And depending on how things went, she would eventually work up the nerve to tell Jordan how she felt about him, if he hadn't already figured out that he was the guy she had the crush on. "How about Monday evening after I get home from work?"

"Okay, that sounds like a good start. But before you get your hopes up, I don't think I've ever seen one of these Cyrano de Bergerac schemes work out according to the plan. I'll do my best to help you in any way I can, but if it doesn't work out, you have to promise me that you won't be upset with me."

Maddy laughed. "Okay. I won't be upset with you. But I have a feeling that this time around, the outcome is going to surprise you." She impulsively squeezed his hand, then jumped out of the car. As she walked to the door, she whispered, "Yes, this time I think you'll be very surprised."

⚜

Jordan's stomach tightened. Again. His stomach had acted strangely the entire ride back to Maddy's house. Trying to shrug it off, he waved good-bye to Maddy, who was standing at her front door, then he walked next door to his parents' house. They weren't home, so he deposited Hancock in the backyard, making a mental note to call his parents later to make sure they knew the puppy was out there. As he started the drive home, he reflected on what had turned out to be an eventful day. He had been excited about having the afternoon free in order to spend time with Maddy and to let the puppy burn off some of his boundless energy.

But there was an uneasy feeling in his stomach that had been bugging him since he'd brought up the subject of relationships. He was angry with this guy Arnold, who seemed to be playing with Maddy's heart.

The man was all wrong for her. Jordan couldn't understand why this guy Arnold didn't see what an altogether lovely woman she was. And at the same time, he was relieved that the two of them weren't really a couple.

But beyond that, his emotions were a twisted jumble of *maybe. . . , what if I*—and *I probably shouldn't.*

Would it be entirely rude of him to say to Maddy, "Forget about Arnold. I'm really attracted to you. How do feel about me?" Or would it be more practical for him to take a stance as a friend in whom she could confide about the whole thing? And would it be fair to himself to try and divert her attention from Arnold when she was feeling so vulnerable? Would she momentarily make herself believe that she had feelings for him, then come to her senses later, realizing that she still cared for Arnold?

Jordan drummed his fingers on the steering wheel and shook his head. That wouldn't be fair to himself. He would be crushed if that were to happen.

He sighed. If he had taken the time to get to know her years ago, maybe this wouldn't be happening now. For all he knew, they would have dated throughout high school and college and been married by now.

Married. The thought had a nice ring to it. But why was he even getting his hopes up? Especially now, with this whole situation about the cooking lessons. But the more he thought about it, the more he realized it was what he really wanted.

He wanted Maddy to be his wife. And thanks to his big mouth and constant teasing back in high school, he'd lost out on winning the woman of his dreams. If he'd only been mature enough to recognize it back then. . .back when she had been interested in him.

It was too late to go back and undo the past. But it wasn't too late to be there for her during this situation with Arnold.

As long as Arnold didn't realize what a jewel Maddy was, Jordan was happy to spend every moment he could with her.

All he could do now was hope and pray the Lord would show him a way to show Maddy how much he cared for her without trying to force her to give up on Arnold.

He had wanted to tell her how he felt about her right there in the car, but then she had come up with the plan for him to give her cooking lessons.

Looking back, he figured he should have said no and then stuck to it. But he realized that no matter how silly he would feel if he went along with it, it would give him the perfect opportunity to spend more time with her. And that seemed like the perfect plan for him. Until now. Taking a clearer look at the situation, he knew this was no way to win a woman's heart. Arnold's shadow would always be hanging over him.

Jordan remembered the dreamy look that Maddy had when she talked about Arnold. Would she ever get that look in her eyes when she thought about Jordan? Jordan shook his head. "Not until she gives up on Arnold," he grumbled. He felt like telling Maddy he'd changed his mind about the cooking lessons, but he had already committed himself. And given his past experiences with Maddy, the last thing he wanted to was break his word.

"I guess I'll have to turn it over to You, Lord," he prayed quietly. "I just hope I have enough faith to let You keep the ball in Your hands, even if I start to feel desperate."

seven

Maddy patiently waited for the students to file out of her class-room. Her first day at work had come to a close. *So far, so good,* she told herself. The students seemed to get along with her well and, except for one student, none of them had really given her too much trouble. However, that one student, a girl named Trina, had given Maddy enough problems to rival the rest of the students' willingness to cooperate. It wasn't as though the girl didn't like the classes. In fact, she seemed to enjoy her work, and learned quickly. She spent a good deal of her time questioning everything Maddy told the class to do, making wisecracks, passing notes, and flirting with the guys in the class. And most infuriatingly, whenever Maddy asked her a question, she would say she didn't know the answer. Yet, Trina answered those questions and more on the pop quiz for the day, and had been the only student in the class to get a perfect score on that quiz.

During the lunch break, Maddy had asked Mrs. Calvin about Trina's academic records. Maddy learned that not only did Trina have some of the top grades of any of the students who had applied to the camp, but she had also just graduated as her class valedictorian. Trina had attended the camp the previous year and won numerous awards for her performance. But when Maddy had consulted Irena Phelps, who'd been Trina's instructor the year before, Maddy learned Trina had been somewhat of a problem student back then.

After the last student left the classroom, Maddy gathered her purse and walked to the parking lot. The camp was being held on a small college campus, which was comprised of no more than ten academic halls connected by scenic, winding pathways. The Mevlom Institute was only using three of the buildings for its camp, and Maddy had only seen the building where she taught her class and the smaller building that housed the campus cafeteria.

As she walked, she noticed a group of students who had been in her classes, including Trina. As she got closer, they suddenly grew quiet and kept casting glances in Maddy's direction. Maddy felt the tiniest sinking sensation in her chest.

Just four years ago, she had been the same age as these students, and there was no way they would have reacted to her then as they just had. Now she was out of the loop, no longer a peer, but an authority figure. *And I'm not even that old,* Maddy thought. *On the other hand, maybe it's a good thing they see me as being so much older. That way, I get more respect when I'm trying to teach. Yes. I'm not here to hang out with them. I'm supposed to be their teacher.*

" 'Bye, Ms. Thompson," said one of the students, a girl named Stacia. Then several of the others in the group followed suit, echoing a chorus of " 'Bye, Ms. Thompson."

Maddy nodded and waved, hoping she was acting in a mature manner. "Good-bye, students," she said, internally wincing. When did she ever really talk like that? In trying to act maturely, she ended up feeling ridiculous. Maddy's cheeks began to grow warm, so she quickened her pace and passed the group, not wanting to overhear what they might say about her.

"Hey, Ms. Thompson?" asked an all too familiar voice. Maddy held back a shudder, realizing there was only one student she knew by voice after her first day on the job. She paused and turned around to see Trina break from the ranks and walk toward her.

Maddy stood and waited for the girl to come closer. But Trina only covered half of the distance between them. Then she all but shouted, "The guys want to know how old you are," as she gestured to some of the boys in the group, who were standing in poses they probably assumed were mature and macho, but actually looked comical.

Maddy didn't know what to say. Why did all the problems

develop after classes were out? She vaguely remembered that some of the guys in her own high school had developed crushes on female teaching assistants and substitutes from local colleges. The girls had been jealous of them, and the guys had swooned when the female teaching assistants walked into a room. The same concept applied to male college students who worked as teaching assistants. The guys got jealous, while the girls had thought they themselves were falling in love.

Maddy had always thought the concept was pretty ridiculous. Some of those college students were only two or three years older than the students they were teaching. And now, she was in the same boat. She frantically dug into her memory to recall what those assistants had done to halt any student's crushes. Unfortunately, she didn't remember. But she knew she had to come up with an answer. Soon.

"I don't think that's really important," she told the students. "What's important is that I'm your teacher for the summer and that means—"

"Did you go to college?" interrupted Trina, who was walking closer to her.

Maddy swallowed and lifted her chin a tad higher. "Yes. And I graduated also." *That sounded pretty silly,* she chided herself.

She heard one of the kids say, "Ooooh, she graduated." The others snickered in response.

What she wanted to do was run to her car, but she couldn't exactly run away from a student, so she stood her ground as Trina grew closer.

When Trina finally got within three feet, Maddy cleared her throat and asked, "Is there something you need?"

Trina turned and looked at her friends who now seemed to be engrossed in conversation. "Um. . .do you think I can talk to you before class on Wednesday?" she asked in a low tone.

Maddy shook her head before she even said a word. She needed to set boundaries before things got out of hand, and the first thing she needed to do was make it clear to Trina and the others that she was in charge. "I really don't think so," she told the girl.

"What about after class, then?" The expression on the girl's face had grown serious, almost pleading and her eyes mirrored the same emotion.

"Well. . . ." Maddy had the feeling whatever she wanted to discuss was important, and she didn't want to turn her down. While she deliberated a moment, she noticed Trina kept turning around to glance at her friends.

Finally, Trina sighed and said, "Never mind. I just thought you meant what you said this morning about talking to you if we needed help and everything. If you don't have time, then I'll talk to somebody else." She turned around to go back to her friends.

Maddy felt terrible. What kind of teacher was she? "All right," she relented before the girl got too far away. "I can stay for fifteen minutes after class on Wednesday. Okay?"

Trina just nodded and jogged over to her friends.

As Maddy resumed the walk to her car, she heard one of the students call out, "Hey, Trina, what'd you say to Ms. Thompson?"

Maddy heard Trina laugh in response and say, "I just told her that her clothes were out of style." The group burst into loud, raucous laughter.

Maddy quickened her pace. That girl was impossible. The second she'd started to feel like she was making a connection, the girl turned around and mocked her in front of the rest of the students.

And, she thought, looking down at her black crepe pantsuit, *this outfit is not out of style. It might be a little dressy, but it's not outdated.*

When she reached her car, she was thoroughly upset. Before she even fastened her seat belt, she took five minutes to pray and calm down so she wouldn't let her emotions affect her driving. When she began to relax, she buckled up and started the car. By the time she got closer to home, she wasn't upset; but she was pretty disheartened, and had serious doubts about whether or not she would be able to teach the rest of the summer.

Her mother was out in the front yard, digging in her flower beds, and Mrs. Myston was helping her.

Maddy parked in the driveway and walked around to the front to say hello.

"How was work?" her mother asked.

"Okay, I guess. I had a little trouble toward the end, but it'll be under control by the end of the week, I'm sure."

Her mother nodded in agreement. "Just give it a little time. I'm sure you'll do a great job."

"I hope so. Otherwise, I might have to find a new job next week."

"If you got the job, I'm sure you can do it. Otherwise, they wouldn't have hired you," her mother said.

Mrs. Myston shook her head. "No offense, Madison, but aren't you a little young to be teaching high school students? What could the people who hired you have been thinking?"

Maddy bristled, but tried to remain calm as she asked, "What do you mean?"

Mrs. Myston patted Maddy's arm in what she probably thought was a comforting manner. "You're just a child yourself. And a nice, well-mannered one at that. What can they expect you to do for those hooligans?"

Maddy wondered if she'd just been insulted. She decided to shake it off, since she knew Mrs. Myston meant well. "Mrs. Myston, these kids are not hooligans. They're some of the brightest and smartest at their schools. I just probably need better teaching skills."

Mrs. Myston shook her head. "You be careful, Madison. I watch the news and I know that smart doesn't always mean 'nice' when it comes to these kids nowadays. You never know what they might be up to."

No one said anything for a minute, then Mrs. Myston brightened and said, "But I do think it's nice of you to try to look for the good in all of your students. That's a good start as long as you don't let your guard down."

"That's true," said her mother. "Maddy always seeks out the best in people," she said smiling.

If only you knew how I feel about Trina right now, Maddy thought. She said, "I guess I'll go in and change. I'll see you later, Mrs. Myston."

"Oh, look, Madison. Your gentleman friend is here," reported Mrs. Myston.

Maddy turned around to see that Jordan had pulled into his parents' driveway. He got out of his car and jogged over, carrying a grocery bag. He handed the bag to Maddy and said, "I'll be over in about ten minutes. I just need to say hi to my parents. But don't peek in the bag."

Maddy stared at the brown paper bag. "What's in here?" she called to Jordan.

Jordan stopped and smiled. "Lesson one. Wife class 101. Don't tell me you forgot."

"Oh. No, I didn't forget, I just didn't realize the semester was starting today." Maddy laughed.

"Wife class?" echoed her mother and Mrs. Myston. The looks on their faces were priceless, and if she hadn't had such a hard day, Maddy might have had a good laugh.

"It's a long story," said Maddy. "And kind of a joke, that I didn't think he would take seriously. But basically, he's teaching me how to cook. So I'd better get inside and make sure the kitchen is clean."

Maddy left the two women out on the lawn and hurried inside to give the kitchen a once-over. She transferred a few items from the sink into the dishwasher and wiped down the counters for good measure. Just as she was finishing, Jordan came through the back door.

"I didn't think you were really going to help me out," Maddy told him.

"I promised I would, didn't I?"

"Well, yeah, but I thought you did it just to make me feel

better. To be honest, I'd pretty much forgotten about it."

Jordan looked a little disappointed. "If you really don't want me to stay, I don't have to."

"No, no. It's okay. I'm ready to learn," said Maddy as she took a seat at the kitchen table.

"Are you wearing that?" Jordan asked.

Maddy looked down at her outfit for the second time that day and sighed. "You think it's outdated, too?" she asked Jordan.

"No, it looks great on you. But it might be a little fancy for cooking class," he said.

"I'll change," said Maddy.

She ran to her room and changed into a T-shirt and pair of shorts, then returned to the kitchen where Jordan had set out several bowls.

He looked up at Maddy. "From now on, I'll let you get all the utensils and things out, but since you were tardy today, I had do it myself," he said in a mock stern voice.

Maddy smiled. "Sorry, Mr. Sanders. I won't be late next time."

Jordan laughed and opened the bag. "Now, the first thing about cooking is you have to follow the directions. If you follow the recipe, it should turn out perfectly. So. . . ." he reached into the bag and pulled out a bag of chocolate chips. "What I want you to do is read over this recipe," he said, handing her the bag.

Maddy took the bag and glanced at the recipe on the back. "We're making cookies? That's it?" she said.

"I thought we'd start off with something easy," he replied.

"Jordan, I thought this was supposed to be beneficial to me. You know, 'wife class' and everything. What man would want to eat cookies for dinner?"

He shrugged. "I would."

Maddy tilted her head and lifted her eyebrows in response. "Every day?"

"If that was all my wife knew how to cook, I would happily

eat cookies day after day after day." He laughed.

"Seriously. I'm sure I can pull off a batch of cookies. When do we get to the harder stuff?"

"After we make these cookies. And I hope for my sake that you can pull this recipe off, because I need these to take to my church's singles' group meeting tomorrow night."

Maddy looked up at him, surprised. "I didn't know you went to your church's singles' group meetings."

He shrugged. "I told you I hang out with them sometimes, but I usually don't make it to the Tuesday night meetings."

"So you're starting now?"

"When I can. They're having a barbecue tomorrow and I'm signed up to bring cookies, so I hope you do a good job, or they'll think I'm an awful cook."

"I'll try my best; but isn't it unethical to try to pass your student's work off as your own?"

"Why don't you tell me?" he laughed. "Between the two of us, you're the one who gets paid to teach."

"Okay, let's get off the subject of teaching. I'd rather not think about it. What do we do first?"

"First, you read the recipe over thoroughly and then get out all of the ingredients. But since they're my cookies for my meeting, I went ahead and bought the ingredients, so all you need to do in this case is take everything out of the bag. However, we will need to use your oven, bowls, and things like that."

"You can be sure I'll deduct the cost from my tuition," she told him. Maddy read the recipe and measured the ingredients while Jordan watched.

Thankfully, the recipe was not very difficult. It actually turned out to be pretty simple, leaving her to wonder why she had previously thought cooking to be some great mystery.

Cooking was turning out to be a combination of math and science, with certain amounts of particular ingredients combining to create edible results. It reminded her of chemistry. Cooking was something she could learn if she really tried.

The only thing that bugged her was the fact that Jordan was taking *her* cookies to his church meeting. *Was he interested in a woman there? And what was he going to tell her about the cookies? 'My cooking student, who has a crush on me, made these. She's not a very good cook, so eat them at your own risk.'*

The thought of it made Maddy a little queasy. But before she became too ill, Jordan interrupted her thoughts.

"So how was your first day at work?"

"It was okay until it was officially over. I had one problem student, but she didn't really get out of hand during class."

"So what happened afterwards?"

Maddy related the events with Trina and the other students and waited for Jordan to respond.

"That was it?" was all he said.

"What do you mean 'it'?" she asked.

"That's not too awful."

"Maybe it's not to you, but to me it is. I have a student who makes fun of me and challenges me in front of the others, and some of the boys have a crush on me."

Jordan gasped loudly, then put his hand across his forehead and clutched the countertop as though he might fall down. "Oh, no! The world is ending! Half of Maddy's students are in love with her and the other half are laughing at her! What to do, what to do!" he said in a high-pitched voice.

"Oh, be quiet," Maddy said, as she playfully tapped him on the arm with the spoon she was using to stir the cookie dough.

"Oops!" Maddy exclaimed, realizing she had gotten some cookie dough on his arm and the sleeve of his shirt.

Jordan instantly sobered. "Hey. This mix is supposed to go in the oven, not on my arm."

"You deserved it."

"I did?"

Maddy nodded.

"Then, I think you deserve this," he said as he wiped some of the dough off his arm and spread it over her nose.

"Very funny," Maddy said. She picked up the spoon and held it in front of her like she was wielding a weapon. "If you want any of this dough to end up in the oven, I suggest you refrain from smearing any more on your student's nose."

"Okay, okay." Jordan backed away in retreat with his hands in the air. "So tell me more about this camp," he said, changing the subject. "I get the feeling it's not your typical summer camp with cabins, mess halls, and macaroni necklaces."

Maddy shook her head. "It's a mix between an internship and a specialized summer camp for high school juniors and seniors who want to go into communications. Some want to work at newspapers, some want work for radio or television, and the camp tries to match them up with businesses in those different fields. They either attend classes or work for eight hours a day, depending on which day it is. Seniors attend the classes Monday, Wednesday, and Friday. Tuesdays and Thursdays they work at the places where they're required to intern. My job is to teach different computer skills that they might need for these kinds of jobs. It's not really complicated, since so many of them have worked with computers a lot. But, every once in a while, I manage to come up with something they don't know. On Tuesdays and Thursdays, I teach the juniors. Wednesdays and Fridays they work at the places where they're interning."

"So what do the juniors do on Mondays?"

"They have the option of either auditing the senior classes or just taking the day off. I only saw two juniors today."

"That's a pretty intense way to spend the summer. Do you think they're having any fun?"

"Probably. I did a similar program during my junior and senior summers. I liked it better than school because I got experience working at big companies, and I didn't have to study subjects I didn't really care for."

"Like home economics," Jordan supplied.

"Yeah."

"Plus, it's not really for the entire summer. The session

ends the second week of August, so they have a little time to unwind before school starts."

"So that's why I never saw you around during the summertime," Jordan said.

"Were you looking for me? Or looking *out* for me to avoid me?" Maddy teased.

"Oh, that's harsh," Jordan said. "Let's get these in the oven." He handed her a cookie sheet.

He noticed I wasn't around in the summer. I wonder what that means, thought Maddy. She wanted to press the question a little further, but Jordan didn't appear to be very talkative at the moment, so she focused on rolling the dough into perfect little balls, then placing them on the baking sheet.

A few minutes later, Jordan spoke up. "You always were so smart, Maddy. Even though I was older, I felt stupid next to you a lot of the time. I barely concentrated in high school and I have the grades to prove it, even though I probably could have done better if I'd worked a little harder." He laughed. "I guess we're total opposites. You liked math and science and hated the other subjects. I liked anything that didn't have absolutes and right and wrong answers, things that change and things that are open to interpretation."

"Like art," she said.

"Exactly. I mean look at us, even now. You're rolling the cookie dough into perfect spheres, and I'm flinging it on the sheet any kind of way."

Maddy looked down at the cookie sheet and chuckled. He was right. "I guess you're right. But even with all our differences, we still get along pretty well, don't you think?"

"Yeah. I guess that's the part I didn't understand back in high school," he said softly.

Before Maddy even realized what he was doing, Jordan leaned over and gently kissed her on her forehead. She looked up at him and held his gaze for a long moment, hoping for some type of profession of love from him. He said nothing, but continued to look into her eyes. Maddy placed her hand on his arm. "Is everything okay?" she said quietly.

Jordan grinned, and seemed to return to his usual joking self. "I guess we need to finish these cookies," he told her. Quickly, he picked up the cookie sheet and put it in the oven. He stayed at the stove for a few minutes, checking the temperature, while Maddy reflected on the kiss. It had happened so fast she wasn't even sure if it was real or if she had imagined it.

What was going on? How could he act like nothing had just happened? Somehow, she was going to have get some answers from him. And the sooner, the better. After a few minutes of shaping more cookie dough, she finally worked up the nerve to look at Jordan who was now busy running water into the sink to wash dishes.

He turned around and flashed her a quick smile. "Now comes the fun part. The cleanup. Do you want to wash or dry?"

"It doesn't matter to me," she said.

"Then you can dry." He turned his back to her and started washing the dishes they'd used.

Maddy silently dried the dishes, and by the time they finished, the first batch of cookies was done. Half were perfect little circles and the other half were wildly abstract shapes.

"Mine look better," said Maddy.

"They look better to you. I think mine have lots of character," he said.

Jordan suggested they take some out to Mrs. Myston and her mother.

"But what about the rest of the dough? I've already started shaping it," she told him.

"Oh, yeah. I guess we should make the rest of them."

"Why don't you take some outside, and I'll get the second batch started," she suggested.

"Good idea. Are you sure you can handle it?"

Maddy rolled her eyes. "I just did these, didn't I?"

"Right." He placed a few cookies on a plate and bounded out the door with a relieved look on his face.

Once again, he seems glad to get away from me, Maddy

thought, recalling the night out on the porch after she'd messed up the vinaigrette.

Maddy put a dozen more cookies on the sheet and checked the temperature of the oven. She set the timer on her watch and went outside to see how everyone liked the cookies.

"Maddy, these are good," said her mother.

"Thanks," Maddy replied, smiling.

"These are delicious, Madison," said Mrs. Myston. "Jordan must be a good teacher to get this kind of result in only one lesson."

Maddy nodded. "He is a good teacher."

The two women complimented the cookies for a few more minutes, then launched into a discussion about the hedge roses they'd planted the week before.

Maddy and Jordan sat and quietly listened while the two women talked. Jordan still seemed a little uncomfortable, so Maddy stayed quiet to see if he would initiate a conversation.

When the timer on her watch sounded, Maddy jumped up and rushed to the kitchen. The cookies were perfectly browned, so she took them from the oven and put another batch in, after making a slight adjustment to the temperature.

Just as she was about to head back outside, the phone rang. "Hello?"

"Maddy, it's Laina. What are you doing?"

"Baking cookies."

Laina laughed. "No really, what are you doing?"

"I am making cookies. . .with Jordan Sanders," Maddy said, checking to make sure Jordan wasn't within earshot.

"How did this come about?" Laina wanted to know.

"It's a long story that I'll have to tell you about later."

"Like when?" she persisted.

"I don't know. The next time I see you."

"How about tomorrow night?"

"Tomorrow?"

"Yes. Some of the people in our Sunday school class are going out for dinner. We can ride together and you can fill me in on the way."

Maddy frowned. "I don't remember hearing about any of this in church yesterday."

"You didn't. Patty just called me about maybe getting some of the class to help plan a surprise party for Arnold's birthday. So some of us are going out to dinner for a little planning session."

"Oh, I see. I guess I could try to make it," Maddy said, remembering that Jordan probably wouldn't stop by because he was going to the party with his friends from church.

"You won't *try* to come. You will come. Okay?" said Laina.

Maddy decided to tease her friend a little. "I guess I could show up. But it's not really you I want to see. I'm only coming because it's for such a good cause."

"What's the good cause that means more to you than seeing your best friend who you've blatantly avoided since you got home from college?"

"Arnold's surprise party, of course," Maddy laughed.

"Ahem," Jordan cleared his throat.

Maddy turned around to see him standing by the door. "Oh, I didn't hear you come in."

"I wanted to check on the cookies," he told her.

"Oh. They should be done by now."

"Already?" he asked.

"Yeah. The recipe said to bake at three hundred degrees for twelve minutes, so I turned it up to broil and figured they should be done in about six minutes." At that moment, the timer on her watch went off. "See? I bet they're ready now."

Jordan just stared at her.

To Laina she said, "I've got to let you go, but I'll see you tomorrow. Just be sure you let me know what time you're picking me up." Maddy hung up the phone and opened the oven door. Thick, black smoke poured out from the interior.

Maddy inhaled smoke and started coughing. "Oops," she said to Jordan.

Jordan grabbed the pot holders from her and pulled the

cookie sheet from the oven.

The cookies were blackened on the bottoms and around the edges, while the top center portion was still raw.

"Hmm. . . ," said Jordan. "What was that theory you had about the temperature again?"

"Logically speaking, I figured if I doubled the temperature, the cookies would be done in half the time. So I made a mistake," she defended herself.

Jordan shook his head. "This is not algebra, Maddy. It's cooking. You have to follow the directions when you don't know what you're doing."

Maddy felt herself growing angry. She made one little mistake, and now he was treating her like she was a two year old. Not to mention the fact that he'd acted like she had the plague after he kissed her. She grabbed a spatula and started scraping the burnt cookies off the cookie sheet. "I know what I'm doing. . .I just made a miscalculation. I'll buy you some cookies for your party, just stop talking down to me. I'm an adult, you know."

"You're right. I'm sorry," he said, his voice taking on an edge. "But maybe if you hadn't been so engrossed in planning Arnold's surprise party, my cookies wouldn't be burnt."

"You had no right to eavesdrop on my phone conversation. And I think you should leave Arnold out of this. He's one of the nicest people I know. Besides, he didn't burn your cookies. I did. And I promise you that you won't have to go to your party empty-handed." Maddy went to the pantry and started pulling out ingredients for more cookies. Thankfully, her mother had everything she needed. She turned to Jordan and said, "I can handle this. Why don't you come back in two hours and I'll have them ready for you?"

"I'll be next door if you get done earlier," was all he said before he left.

"Good riddance," Maddy grumbled after he left. "I'll have your cookies ready for the party, mister. You just watch. I'm sure your girlfriend will be impressed."

eight

Jordan stared in the direction of the television set, but his eyes weren't focused on the show his parents were engrossed in watching.

He had really messed things up now. For one thing, what had he been thinking to kiss her like that? And why hadn't he been more sensitive to her feelings about the burnt cookies? Or better yet, why did he overreact when he heard her discussing Arnold's surprise party?

Although he'd known this was going to happen, it just didn't seem fair that Arnold should get all of Maddy's romantic attention, while he had to settle for a cooking-class relationship.

Jordan stood up and walked to the kitchen. He lifted one of the sections in the blinds and peeked out the window. He saw Maddy's outline in her kitchen, moving around. He chuckled softly. She really seemed determined to make those cookies.

Jordan opened the refrigerator and poured a glass of milk. Sitting down at the kitchen table, he thought, *I probably should go and apologize to her*. Otherwise, they would both be upset and nothing would be resolved. He took another swallow and rubbed his hand over his head. Yes, he would go over and apologize, although it would be nice if she would come and apologize to him.

He bowed his head and prayed that he would be able to control his emotions and not get bent out of shape about the little things so much. After all, a few burnt cookies were not the end of the world. And no matter how much he hated to admit it, a party for Arnold wasn't exactly cataclysmic, either. But he didn't want to destroy his somewhat fragile friendship with Maddy.

Suddenly, the light flickered on. Jordan looked up to see

his dad standing over him.

"What in the world are you doing, sitting here in the dark?"

Jordan hesitated. Whereas his mother was slightly more open to hearing about Christianity, his dad was way more resistant. Did his dad really want to know what he'd been doing? Jordan swallowed and decided to be honest. "Actually, I was praying," he told him.

His dad snorted. "Did it help anything?"

"God listens to all of my prayers, Dad. And He answers them, too."

Jordan could tell his dad was already upset about something else and he braced himself for what might be coming next. When his dad got in this mood, he was always ready for a good shouting match about why Jordan had chosen to become a Christian. The two of them would go at it for hours, Jordan trying to make his dad become a Christian, and his father putting down everything Jordan said.

But lately, Jordan had realized it was absolutely hypocritical to yell at his dad about how Christianity had changed him. If he had changed so much, why was he yelling about it? It only infuriated Martin Sanders all the more when Jordan wouldn't yell back at him.

His dad sat down across from him and smiled without warmth. Jordan felt like he was the opposing attorney at one of his dad's trials. When he'd been in high school, many of his friends had been envious of the material things his family owned. But they didn't really know what it had been like to grow up as the only child of Martin Sanders, the champion prosecutor. They didn't know what it felt like to live in a house where everything was conducted like a trial. And they certainly didn't know what it had felt like to tell his dad that he didn't want to follow in his footsteps and go to law school. His dad had ignored him for a week when Jordan had announced his intention to go to art school.

Just when it seemed Martin had starting accepting the idea of his son being an artist, Jordan had come home and announced that he had asked Jesus into his heart. That's when the real opposition had begun.

Jordan sat up straighter and waited for what was coming.

"I notice you're spending a lot of time next door."

Jordan nodded.

"Would you like to share the reason why?"

Jordan swallowed. "The Thompsons' daughter, Maddy. She's a friend of mine."

"Since when? You made fun of her in high school."

"And I apologized, and now we're friends."

"So this was another one of your mercy missions?"

Jordan frowned. "I don't know what you're talking about. Maddy is my friend, plain and simple."

"I thought you Christians are supposed to tell the truth, but here you are telling me you've forgotten all about Harper Blackston?"

Jordan's throat felt like it was swelling. "You didn't ask me about Harper Blackston. You asked me about Maddy. And no, I haven't forgotten about Harper."

"Well, what are you doing with her, Jordan? Is this little project something I'm going to have to write a check for when you come crying to me in the middle of the night?"

Jordan stood up. "You have no right to throw that back at me. It was my own money—"

"You listen to me." His dad had stood up and now stood directly in front of him. "It wasn't your money yet," he yelled. "It was mine, and I made a big mistake when I wrote that check. So whatever you do now, make sure you paint enough Noah's Arks in church hallways to cover any more checks you might feel obligated to write."

"I won't ask you for another cent, you can be sure of that," Jordan said, his voice growing louder.

"While you're at it, why don't you pray and ask for those nightmares to go away? Why don't you pray and ask for that *Christian* counselor to send me back some of the money I shelled out—"

He was interrupted by a knock on the kitchen door.

Jordan hurried over to open the door. Maddy stood outside, holding a plastic bag full of cookies.

"I'm sorry I'm a few minutes late but here they are," she said, holding out the bag. She peeked around Jordan and waved to his dad. "Hi, Mr. Sanders," she said. "I hope I didn't come at a bad time."

"No, of course not," said his dad. "Those cookies look delicious. I hope Jordan will let me taste a few."

Jordan was irritated with the way his dad always acted like the model father when other people were around. He smiled at Maddy and said, "I'm sorry I got upset about the burnt cookies, and I really appreciate you making these."

"Oh, it's okay." She smiled. "I needed the practice."

Jordan felt his dad's eyes on him and couldn't think of anything to say. Maddy shifted from foot to foot. "Well, I guess I'll see you later?"

"Are you busy tomorrow night?" Jordan asked.

"Actually, I'm supposed to help plan Arnold's party. And I thought you had a barbecue?"

"Oh, that's right. Then maybe sometime later this week. I'll give you a call, okay?"

"Okay," Maddy said, flashing him a tiny smile.

Jordan shut the door and turned around to face his dad. "I'm pretty tired. Is there anything else you need to say?"

His dad shrugged. "You've heard it before, but I'll say it again. I don't like seeing my only son running around being a do-gooder. There was no reason for you to get involved in all this religion stuff. What happened was not your fault."

Jordan let out a weary sigh. "Dad, I know you don't believe it, but being a Christian got me through what happened. I don't know what would have happened to me if I hadn't. . . ." He trailed off, not wanting to pursue the subject anymore. He leaned over and hugged his dad, who instantly stiffened. His dad had never been the hugging type. "I'll just say this. I love you and mom, and I'll pray for you until the day I die. Jesus is just waiting for you to say yes, and when you do, you'll know true peace."

His dad said nothing, but instead turned out the light and left the room.

Jordan quietly left and drove home. He hadn't really gotten to apologize to Maddy the way he'd wanted, but he had done the best he could, given the circumstances. What made him restless were the memories his dad had exultantly dredged up and waved in front of him like a trophy.

That night, he tossed and turned, unable to rest. When he did surrender to exhaustion, his sleep was plagued with a montage of guilt and anguish.

nine

Wednesday afternoon, Maddy walked to her car after work. Unlike Monday, she didn't see any sign of her students, and she was relieved. They had been a little more difficult today, and she was glad to be going home. Maddy opened the back door of her car and threw her bags on the back seat. Just as she opened the front door, she heard a voice.

"Hey, Ms. Thompson!"

Maddy turned around and saw Trina running towards her.

As the girl came closer, she slowed down a bit. "You said you would talk to me today after class, Ms. Thompson."

Maddy looked at her watch. "I promised you fifteen minutes. As it stands, classes have been out for almost half an hour. I was waiting in the classroom for you to show up, but you never did. I assumed you had changed your mind." Maddy tried to look pleasant, but she was frustrated that the girl still wanted to have this discussion.

Trina looked down at the ground, then back up at Maddy. "I kind of forgot, okay? So can we talk now?"

Maddy held back the enormous sigh she wanted to release, and pointed to a small wooden bench a few feet away. "Over there," she told Trina. "But I still only have fifteen minutes."

Once they were seated, Maddy asked, "Now, what was it you wanted to discuss?"

Trina suddenly seemed hesitant to speak, which Maddy deemed to be uncharacteristic of the girl, even after having been her teacher for a short time. Usually, she seemed to be the center of attention.

Finally, she said, "I just wanted to ask you, well. . .how did you get along with people in college?"

Maddy was surprised. All of this for such a simple question?

"Well, I guess I got along with everyone pretty well."

"But how did you make friends?"

"I just. . .did my best to be myself, and tried to reach out to people. Especially my freshman year. Everyone is trying to make friends then, so it's not too hard." She smiled at Trina. "Are you worried about making friends this fall?"

The girl shrugged. "A little. I don't have too many friends right now."

Maddy was surprised. Every time she saw Trina, she was with a large group of the other students. Cautiously, she said, "It looks like you're getting along with the kids here at camp."

Trina shrugged. "Not really. They like it when I make jokes or help them with their homework. Nobody ever calls me up and invites me to go anywhere. The boys will flirt with me for a while. The girls will be jealous because the boys are interested in me. Then the boys will find out I'm smart and back off. The girls might be nicer to me after a while, but they don't ever really count me as a friend."

"Is that why you pretend you don't know the answers in my class?"

Trina nodded. "Most of the people here this year are new, and they've never met me before. At least they'll be friends with me for a little while."

Maddy bit the inside of her lip. She knew that feeling all too well. But she didn't think she'd experienced half as much as Trina had. Although Jordan and his friends had teased her mercilessly, she'd still had plenty of other friends, both male and female. From what she could tell, most of Trina's peers had alienated her. Maddy was at a loss for words. She knew that she couldn't honestly tell Trina, "I know what you're going through." But she couldn't just say, "I'm sure everything will work out someday," either.

Quickly, Maddy prayed before she spoke. *Lord, please help me to say the right thing. I don't know exactly how she feels, but I have an idea. Show me how to tell her about You and how You care for her.*

Trina was staring at her, waiting for an answer. She seemed like a different girl than the one Maddy had dealt with during classes. She was serious, mature, respectful. . .and hurt.

"You know, Trina, I think at college you'll be able to have a fresh start. But I don't think you should try to reinvent yourself, even temporarily, just to make people like you."

"But nobody will talk to me if I don't, Ms. Thompson."

"I think that if you let people know you're smart and you're not ashamed of it, they will learn to respect you, even if they are a little jealous or intimidated."

"They never have before," Trina said.

"Well, that was their loss. I think you should concentrate on trying to be yourself instead of trying to be what you think people would like for you to be."

Trina shrugged. "But what if they still don't like me after that?"

Maddy took a deep breath. "Trina, did you know that Jesus loves you? Even if you feel like no one else cares, Jesus does."

Trina stood up. "Listen, Ms. Thompson. I came to talk to you because you're not much older than me and you're really smart. I thought you might be able to help me out and give me advice about making friends. What I don't need is a Sunday school lesson. I thought you were pretty cool, but you sound like a preacher." With that, Trina walked away.

Maddy wondered whether or not she should chase Trina, but she decided against it. She didn't know if she had broken any kind of rules by witnessing to Trina, but it might make matters worse if she went running after her, so she just prayed that Trina would be okay until Friday. Maybe then she would have a chance to talk to her again.

Maddy waited for several more minutes in case Trina came back, but she didn't return. Reluctantly, Maddy got in her car and drove home. She decided to watch her mother cook dinner in order to gain a little cooking practice. After dinner, she graded some of the students' work and prepared lessons for the next week. She tried to relax by reading a book, but she felt restless.

After almost an hour of rereading the same page of the novel, she decided to call Jordan and see what he was up to. She hadn't seen him since Monday night, and she didn't get to talk to him for very long after she finished the cookies because he had been having a discussion with his dad. Or maybe it had been an argument. What she did know was that she could hear the shouting even in her own backyard.

She searched around in her room for his phone number and then dialed. The phone rang four times, and just as she was going to hang up, he answered.

"Hello?" His voice sounded groggy, almost as if he had been asleep.

"Hi, Jordan, it's Maddy."

"Hi." He sounded a little down. "Is there something you need?"

"Well. . .not really. I was just calling to say hello. I hadn't heard from you in a couple of days, and I was just wondering if you were okay."

He waited a long time before answering. Finally, he said, "What do you mean by okay?"

"I–I overheard your dad yelling the other night."

"What did you hear?" he wanted to know.

"Nothing, really." Maddy was a little embarrassed. She probably shouldn't have said anything. She'd be embarrassed if someone overheard her parents fussing at her. "I didn't hear anything. I just heard loud voices," she told him.

Jordan sighed deeply. "I don't know if I've told you this before, but my parents aren't Christians. So every once in a while, my dad decides to prove how wrong I am about being saved."

"Oh, Jordan, I'm really sorry. I don't have any idea how that might feel."

He was quiet. "Be glad you don't know what it's like. It's not much fun."

"Is there anything I can do?" she asked, feeling helpless.

"Just pray."

"Consider it done," she told him.

"Are you busy Saturday?" he asked.

"Not that I know of."

"Then let's do something."

"Like what?"

"How about I surprise you?"

Maddy laughed. "That sounds like fun. What time should I be ready?"

"How about ten?"

"In the morning?"

"Yep. In the morning."

"I take it you're already formulating some type of plan," she said. "Can you give me a hint?"

"I don't know. I don't want to give it away."

"Come on. . .just a little clue?"

"Okay. You might want to bring a camera."

"That's it?"

"That's all the hints you get. You won't find out anything else until Saturday."

Maddy laughed. "Okay. I guess I'll just have to wait until Saturday."

A few moments later, Maddy ended the conversation and hung up the phone. She exhaled softly. Jordan was trying terribly hard to pretend that he was okay, but he wasn't. She could tell something was bothering him, but whatever it was, he didn't want to talk about it.

Lord, please give him peace about what's bothering him and heal what needs to be healed.

ten

Saturday morning, Maddy awoke early and patiently waited for Jordan, who came to her house five minutes early. His surprise turned out to be a "tour" of sorts, during which they visited several of Kansas City's many fountains. At each fountain, they took pictures of each other, and when they reached the final destination, the famous J. C. Nichols Fountain on the Plaza, they sat in the grass and had a picnic.

Maddy invited Jordan to join her at her church on Sunday, but he seemed to grow uncomfortable and declined, saying he'd prefer not to. Monday morning she returned to work and found that Trina was no longer being disruptive in class. In fact, she had become the total opposite. She was quiet and withdrawn, and during free periods, she no longer spent time with the other kids. Instead, she would retreat to a corner and just sit or read a book. Maddy noticed that the other kids seemed puzzled at first by Trina's behavior, but as time passed, they began teasing the girl, calling her names.

Maddy was shocked to see that the kids had turned on Trina so quickly. Just a few weeks earlier, she'd been the center of attention, and everyone had seemed to enjoy her company. Now, it was just the way Trina had complained to Maddy. When she showed the other kids that she was intelligent, then they didn't seem to think she was much fun.

Maddy instantly identified with how Trina must have felt, but when she tried to talk to the girl, Trina told her to stay away from her. "I don't need you feeling sorry for me, Ms. Thompson. I already told you it would happen," she said. From then on, she seemed to purposefully avoid Maddy and rarely even made eye contact with her.

As the rest of June unfolded, Maddy was happy that

Jordan seemed to spend more and more time dropping by her house in the evenings. They spent hours cooking. And while Jordan proved to be a patient teacher, Maddy felt she was a good student. He complimented her many times on her ability to pick up on things quickly. She made mistakes on occasion, but she rarely made the same mistake twice.

Over the Fourth of July weekend, Jordan traveled with Maddy's family to St. Louis where her brother-in-law Max's relatives lived. Max's family was a lot of fun, and their holiday get-togethers were very lively. She and Jordan endured lots of good-natured teasing about the status of their relationship. Soon everyone lost interest when Mavis, Stacy's new mother-in-law, along with Maddy and Stacy's own mother brought up the subject of Max and Stacy starting a family.

Although Maddy could tell Stacy wasn't thrilled with all of the attention, Stacy and Max took it in stride. Maddy was just glad the focus had shifted from herself and Jordan, because the last thing she wanted was for Jordan to feel pressure about their relationship. And as far as she could tell, he didn't get upset. He continued coming over to visit, and the two went on several outings together, although Jordan assured her they were going just "as friends." It wasn't exactly the most romantic summer of her life, but Maddy didn't complain. She kept praying and waiting for an opportunity to tell Jordan how she really felt about him.

But shortly afterward, Maddy had to deal with more pressing concerns. Trina's grades started dropping dramatically, and the girl began skipping classes. On the rare occasion that Trina did come to class, she totally avoided Maddy and the other kids. Finally, Maddy reported to Mrs. Calvin what was going on, but her supervisor advised Maddy not to get involved in students' disagreements. "We're not here to make everyone get along," the older woman told Maddy. "Our job is to teach. Kids have arguments all of the time. Chances are, next week Trina will be back in the group, and they'll all be teasing some other kid. We can't spend our time trying to make kids like each other. They have to learn to solve their own problems in a mature way."

Maddy tried to explain that she knew how Trina was feeling, but Mrs. Calvin just waved her off. "As long as she's not a problem in the classroom, it's not really your problem, Maddy. If she does something that warrants discipline, then we can do more. We might be able to call a conference with her parents or something, and get more insight into what's going on at home. But remember, we're not psychologists, we're teachers. If we spent our time trying to reach out to all the kids who have felt rejected at one time or another, we'd never get any teaching done. It happens to almost everyone at some time or another."

And it can hurt for a long time, Maddy thought. But in her heart, she knew Mrs. Calvin was right. Most kids in school felt like outcasts at some time or another, but eventually they resolved their problems. And even though she had only been hired to teach, Maddy's heart ached for the pain Trina was feeling and she wished she could do something to help the girl.

❧

A few days later, during one of her cooking sessions with Jordan, Maddy mentioned the situation with Trina.

When she told him about the other kids making fun of Trina, Jordan seemed to grow uneasy.

Frowning, he said, "Does she seem like she's angry at the other kids?"

Maddy shrugged. "I don't think so. Hurt is more what I'm thinking. I just keep wondering if there's a way I can help her. Maybe I was too unfeeling the day she came to me for advice. I basically just threw out some pat answers at her and told her to be herself, because eventually, someone who cares about what's inside will come along and be her friend." Maddy looked at Jordan and said, "I think I felt like her sometimes in high school, and I used to get so tired of hearing people say, 'eventually somebody will like you for who you really are.' And now, I've gone and told someone else that same answer. I feel like such a hypocrite."

Jordan crossed his arms and leaned against the wall. "You know, hearing this from you makes me feel pretty bad, too. I know I've apologized for my teasing, but I can't apologize for the people who teased you because they heard me do it. I feel so responsible for how hurt you felt."

Maddy chuckled softly. "Jordan, I appreciate your honesty and remorse, but I don't hold any of that against you. Sure, you might have given some other people the idea to tease me, but whether you made fun of me or not, somebody was probably going to pick on me at some time or another." She paused, then finished. "And as much as I'm embarrassed to admit it, I did my own share of teasing people who I figured were lower on the totem pole than myself. I don't think anyone is innocent of that, but I really wish people would think more about the consequences before they ridicule someone else."

"Yeah. . .the consequences," Jordan murmured. He tilted his head to the side and asked, "You don't think she wants to get back at the other kids, do you?"

"No, I think she'd rather just disappear so they won't have anything to say about her. I just keep thinking that there's something I could do to help her."

Jordan shook his head vigorously. "Promise me you won't get involved with this, Maddy. Just like your boss said, you're just a teacher, and it's not part of your job to fix your students' arguments."

Maddy frowned. "Jordan, I don't think you're being very sensitive to how she feels. If I can figure out a way to help her, I will."

"No! Just stay out of it."

Maddy was stunned. In all the years she'd known him, he had never yelled at her. Even all of his teasing had been done in a lighthearted tone of voice. She didn't know what to say, so she waited for him to speak.

Jordan walked over and stood directly in front of her. "You have to promise me that you will stay out of this. Let the kids work it out themselves."

Maddy was too shaken by his previous outburst to argue with him. Silently, she nodded.

Jordan sighed with what seemed to be relief, but he still seemed uncomfortable. He fixed himself a glass of water, then sat down at the kitchen table.

Something was still disturbing him, and he didn't appear willing to share it with her just yet. But it didn't look like he felt like continuing their cooking lesson, either. Maddy nervously cleared her throat and Jordan looked at her expectantly. "You know, I'm a little tired from work," she said. "Would it be okay with you if we finish this tomorrow?" She looked around the kitchen. So far, they had only measured out dry ingredients for a loaf of focaccia. It would keep just fine until tomorrow.

Jordan nodded in agreement. "If you don't mind, I think that's a good idea." He stood up and moved toward the back door. "But I just remembered that I can't come tomorrow. Remember, I'm moving in two days and even though I don't have that much stuff, I've still got to pack it."

"I don't envy you one bit," Maddy said, hoping to lighten the mood. "It took me long enough to get everything packed to bring home from school. You need any help?"

"Nah. I'll be done in a couple of evenings, I think. And don't you have to get ready for Arnold's party this weekend?"

Maddy shrugged. "Yeah, you're right. In fact, I'm baking the cake, so pray for me. I'll be really embarrassed if it doesn't turn out right."

"Hey, you've been a good student. You make me proud."

"Thanks," she grinned. "But I'm looking to brush up on my painting skills, so when you decide how you're going to decorate your loft, I'll be glad to lend a hand."

Jordan eyed her carefully. "So now you want this guy to know that you're a skilled wall painter?"

Maddy didn't answer for a minute. Jordan had a habit of bringing up this guy she had a crush on and making her feel flustered. She couldn't tell if he knew she was referring to him and he was gently teasing her, or if he thought she was referring to someone else. Either way, she didn't want to just blurt things out one day. She was going to have to tell him. . . eventually.

"Ahem. Maddy, I'm willing to let you help me, but remember I have to live there, and paint can be kind of expensive. Plus, the place has wood floors which I prefer stayed unpainted. So let's try not to relive any of your early kitchen mishaps in my apartment."

Maddy grinned widely. "I'm not clumsy, you know. I just have little accidents sometimes. But I promise I'll be very careful with your paint and your precious hardwood flooring. So when do we start?"

"I'm moving on Friday. Give me a few days to get settled in. How about a week from today?"

"Okay, I'll have to check with Stacy or Laina and see if one of them can come. If one of them can, we'll see you next Wednesday."

Jordan lifted an eyebrow. "Stacy or Laina?"

"Mm-hmm. I know we're just friends and everything, but that's been my little personal rule all through college. If I'm going to a guy's house, I need to have someone there with me. You understand, right?"

"Oh, yeah. I totally understand. And that's a good idea. I should have been the one to think of that," he said. He opened the door to leave, and said, "Next Wednesday, then. I'll probably give you a call sometime before then."

"Okay." Maddy waved as he left.

For the next few minutes, she puttered around the kitchen, putting up the ingredients they'd measured. As she worked, she hummed a little tune, smiling to herself. Things with Jordan were going well. He was proud of her progress in the cooking department, and soon, she was going to show him that she could be a good homemaker.

The only troublesome spot in her plan was the fact that he

kept questioning her about the guy she'd previously admitted to being interested in. He kept dropping hints that he was willing to help figure out what she should tell the guy. Sooner or later, she was going to have to fess up. The only problem was, she didn't want to tell him until she was a little more proficient at becoming more wifely.

As she looked around the room, trying to figure out what to do, the huge calendar on the refrigerator caught her attention.

In a week, July would be over, and Maddy still hadn't worked up the nerve to tell Jordan about her crush on him. She felt boxed in—unwilling to tell him—but frustrated with herself for feeling so nervous about it. Maddy remembered a Scripture Jordan had mentioned several weeks earlier.

The truth will set you free. "You seem like you could use some freedom," he'd joked. And he was right. She wasn't going to experience freedom as long as she kept her mouth shut. Yet, never had there been a moment that seemed like the right time.

"You have to tell him the next time you see him," she admonished herself.

Hopefully, he would take it well. If not, she only had three weeks until her teaching job at the camp ended. If Jordan couldn't stand her, maybe she could move away and get a job in a different city to spare herself the embarrassment of occasionally running into him.

❧

Jordan assembled yet another box and tried to stifle a yawn. It was one o'clock in the morning, and he was supposed to move in another seven or eight hours.

Unfortunately, due to some unforeseen complications on one of his projects, he'd had to put off packing until now. And if he was going to get any rest before morning, he needed to finish soon. Looking around the small living room, he was amazed to see how much stuff he'd accumulated in the few months he'd been living there. And even more amazing was the amount of time it was taking to pack it all up.

At this point, he was simply throwing things into boxes with no set pattern of organization. He would just need to unpack everything pretty soon to make sure he could find all of his essentials.

As he worked, he thought about the conversation he'd had with Maddy a couple of nights earlier. For a moment, he could have imagined that *he* was the guy she had been working so hard to impress. When he'd asked about the mystery man for what seemed to him like the millionth time, something in her eyes had illuminated, causing him to recall the dreamy-eyed look she used to give him in high school. Until then, he hadn't seen that look from her since their reconciliation, unless they were discussing the mystery guy.

At times, he was tempted to believe that the attraction he felt toward her was returned, but most of the time, she was all business. She had a goal in mind, and he still couldn't figure out the exact purpose of the cooking lessons.

And when she'd mentioned she'd be bringing a chaperone to his apartment, he was surprised. At first he thought she might be hinting that she felt some attraction to him, but his hopes had been dashed when she'd told him she had to stick to her rule even though they were "just friends." She wasn't really afraid of being alone with him, because they'd been out dozens of times. But they had always been in public places. And at her house, at least one of her parents was usually around.

She was just politely letting him know that even though she didn't feel anything for him, she just wanted to make sure there was no "appearance of evil" as long as they were at his place.

Probably so Arnold doesn't think she's got a boyfriend or something, Jordan thought.

This Arnold business was getting out of hand. The more time Jordan spent teaching Maddy how to cook, the more equity she was investing in her future with Arnold.

Jordan shook his head. His relationship with Maddy was

turning out to be pretty one-sided. Apparently, he was the only one who was emotionally involved. Something had to give. The next time he saw her, he was going to have to start winding things down. She had developed into a more than adequate cook, and he had already promised that she could help him paint his apartment. But after that, he was going to put an end to all of their time together.

Soon, he would start pressing her to tell Arnold how she felt. And the sooner the better. If Arnold returned her interest, Jordan could gracefully bow out before he got any more emotionally involved with her. And if Arnold didn't. . .Jordan would be there to pick up the pieces.

Yes, that's the way to handle it. The only thing that still concerned him was Maddy's desire to help her wayward student. The eerie similarity of that situation sent chills down his back. Maddy had seemed frightened when he'd suddenly yelled at her, and he'd been too embarrassed to explain his outburst. But if she grew too insistent in trying to reach out to that girl, he was going to have to tell her about Harper Blackston.

He had dreaded doing so because, given his own rocky past with Maddy, he wondered whether she would be able to forgive him for the part he'd played in the whole ordeal.

Jordan set his jaw grimly. As things stood, there was probably no future for him and Maddy, and he was already coming to terms with that. But if he needed to protect Maddy's safety, he'd tell her the whole story without worrying about whether she would think less of him. Her life was too important to risk his own discomfort.

eleven

Wednesday evening, Maddy drove downtown with Laina to Jordan's loft. Laina was hardly thrilled with the prospect of coming along since lately, she and Maddy rarely saw one another outside of church events, due to their busy work schedules and Maddy's many friendly get-togethers with Jordan.

The only image Laina held of Jordan was of the cocky, teasing flirt he'd been in high school. And now, whenever Maddy brought up the subject of Jordan, Laina changed the subject. Maddy had hoped bringing Laina along for the evening would show her friend what a different person Jordan had become. And secretly, Maddy had decided that Laina would probably be good moral support when she told Jordan the truth about her crush on him.

In the car outside of Jordan's, Laina crossed her arms. "How long do you think we'll be staying?"

Maddy groaned. "I don't know. And if I'd known you were going to be so pouty about this, I wouldn't have asked you to come."

Laina stared at Maddy pointedly. "You knew I didn't want to come and watch you swoon over your old crush, but you had to bring me anyway, because Stacy was busy."

Maddy opened the car door and got out. "I am not swooning over Jordan anymore. We are just friends." She walked briskly toward the entrance of the building.

"But you still like him."

"What if I do?" Maddy challenged.

"I don't want you to get hurt all over again."

Maddy stopped walking. "How many times do I have to tell you that he has changed?"

114

"It's too soon to really tell," Laina insisted. "In high school, he dated so many girls, it made my head swim. And he never felt any remorse about breaking a girl's heart."

"Don't worry about my heart," Maddy reassured her. "He already broke it once, and I will not give him the opportunity to do it again. So just try to be nice to him for my sake, okay?"

"I'll *try*," Laina grumbled.

As they rode the elevator to Jordan's apartment, Maddy contemplated the situation. Bringing Laina along had not been the wisest idea. Instead of making her confession to Jordan, Maddy would have to work to keep the peace between Laina and Jordan. So, her confession would have to wait for another day. Maddy smiled, feeling very relieved. Yes, she decided, she would have to come clean with Jordan some other time. Maybe. If only she could figure out when.

Seconds later, they stepped off the elevator and walked a few feet to Jordan's apartment door. As Maddy was about to knock, he swung the door open. Hancock squeezed his way past Jordan and jumped up to greet Maddy in his usual manner.

"Sit, Hancock." Maddy laughed. "At least your paws aren't all muddy. I think the indoor life is a good thing for you," she said, while ruffling the puppy's ears.

"You're five minutes late," Jordan said, smiling.

"Sorry about that," said Maddy. "We had technical difficulties during our walk from the car to the door." She looked pointedly at Laina. "But everything's fine now."

Turning to Jordan, she said, "Do you remember my friend Laina?"

"Oh, yeah. When I teased you, she was always right there with you to glare at me." He glanced over at Laina, who was standing silently with her arms folded. "And it looks like she's only gotten better at it."

"Laina," Maddy pleaded.

Jordan held out his hand. "C'mon, let's call a truce. I'm a changed man. Really. You don't have to worry about me." Hancock lay on the floor near Laina's feet and rolled over on his back. "See, even Hancock likes you," Maddy said, trying to break the ice. "Please, Laina?"

Laina eyed Jordan a while longer, then reluctantly held out her hand. "I hope you're telling the truth," she told him.

Jordan shook her hand and smiled. "Don't worry, I'll be on my best behavior."

Hancock sat up and barked as if to concur with Jordan. Laina managed a small grin.

Jordan wiped his hand across his brow and said, "Whew." Maddy and Laina stared at him questioningly. Jordan shrugged. "It's pretty nerve-wracking to know somebody who can't stand you is going to help you paint your apartment. Especially if you have floors this beautiful."

Maddy and Laina laughed along with Jordan.

"I think he's the one you'll have to worry about." Maddy pointed at Hancock. "How are you going to keep him out of the paint?"

Jordan grimaced. "Oh, no, I hadn't thought about it. The loft is one huge space, so I can't put him in another room. Come on in, and I'll figure out something," he said, waving them inside. Jordan offered Maddy and Laina some tea while he set up a temporary furniture barricade to keep Hancock away from the painting. Laina played with Hancock while Jordan moved furniture, and she seemed to be having a good time—with the puppy, at least.

Inwardly, Maddy was relieved. Jordan had managed to talk Laina into a truce, making things easier for all of them for the evening. But, she still didn't think now was the time to open her mouth about her crush on him. She'd have to do it sometime when she and Jordan were alone.

As Jordan went off to a corner to collect some cans of paint, Maddy looked around. The room was the size of a basketball court. The apartment was currently nothing but a huge, wide-open room. In addition, there was a small upstairs loft area that was partially hidden from view by a half wall that ran the length of the area, with the exception of the entrance at the top of the short flight of stairs. The walls had probably once been bright white, but had faded and were pretty dingy. The hardwood floors, though, were a beautiful shade of honey brown and had been sanded, stained, and varnished to perfection.

Boxes were stacked in a haphazard fashion throughout the room, and several pieces of furniture sat in the middle of the space, forming the puppy barricade. A kitchen area occupied another corner.

Jordan came and stood next to Maddy as she finished her perusal of his home. "So what do you think?"

"It's beautiful. It really is. I love the natural light."

Jordan nodded. "That's part of the reason I picked this place," he said, gesturing to one of the walls lined with huge windows.

"So how are you planning to arrange your furniture?" Laina wanted to know.

Jordan shook his head. "I'm not quite sure yet. I guess I'll have to find out after the paint dries. Part of the fun with a loft is trying to figure out how you want to divide the living area." He walked to one end of the room and Maddy and Laina followed. He waved his hand toward the kitchen. "As you can see, this is the kitchen, and I plan to leave that space open, instead of walling it off. Right over there, I plan to put the dining area, and over here," he said as he walked toward the middle of the room, "is where I want the main living space to be. Kind of a great room type of area. And then, that big space over there will be my office and studio work space." He grinned. "That way, I'll be able to work on some of my bigger paintings at home."

Maddy smiled. "I bet you're pretty excited about that."

"Definitely."

"But how are you going to divide the areas so they look separate?" Maddy asked. "Right now it still just looks like one big room."

"That's where I get to use my imagination. And paint," he added, grinning. "Eventually, I want to use murals to create a feeling of separation between the spaces. But before I go painting huge pictures, I've got to get the walls painted plain old white. So let's get started, okay?"

"Okay," Maddy agreed.

For the next hour, the three of them worked to ready the walls for painting by taping off the moldings and ceiling, then securing newspapers to the first few feet of floor that extended out from the wall. After that, they got out the paint rollers and proceeded to apply a coat of bright white paint to the walls, with the exception of the one wall that was totally brick.

Maddy had never painted a room in her life, and she discovered it was hard and somewhat messy work. However, she didn't mention her complaints to Jordan because she didn't want him to think she was a wimp.

An hour and a half later, the first coat was complete. Although it was dark outside, Maddy could still see that the new paint was a huge improvement over the dull white the walls had been earlier. She glanced at her watch and realized it was getting late. She would have liked to stay a little longer, but she had to work the next day and she knew Laina had to do the same. She grabbed one of the wet towels Jordan had set aside to use for cleaning and rubbed some of the fresh paint splatters off of her hands.

"Jordan," she said, "I hate to paint and run, but we've got to get home. But I'd love to come back and help again. I'm curious to see what's next."

Jordan paused from painting for a moment. "Thanks. I'm glad you guys helped me. This is a huge room and I really didn't expect to get a whole coat done today." He returned the roller to the rolling pan and walked Maddy and Laina to the door. "And you two are welcome to come back and help out again. I figure I'll let this dry for two or three days, then put the next coat on. After that, we'll have to touch up around the baseboards and the ceiling. Then we paint the trim."

"Sounds like we have lots of work cut out for us," said Maddy.

"Oh, joy," Laina said dryly. At first, Maddy was concerned that Laina wouldn't be willing to come back with her, but as she glanced at her friend, she noticed a playful sparkle in Laina's eyes.

"And thank you, Laina, for helping out, even though I know you'd rather have been somewhere else."

"Oh, it was no problem, really," she said. "Maddy gave me a choice of whether or not I could come." Continuing, she added, "She said I had to come or she wouldn't be my best friend anymore. Naturally, I wanted to keep my best friend, so I came," she deadpanned.

Maddy exhaled loudly in exasperation. "Laina, it wasn't exactly like that," she scolded playfully.

"Maybe not in your memory." Laina laughed. "But it was, and I forgive you for using the ultimatum."

Maddy sighed. "I think it's about time for us to be going. I'll give you a call in a couple of days and see what's going on, okay?"

Jordan nodded in agreement. When Maddy and Laina left, he walked with them to Maddy's car.

On the way home, Laina spent most of the time talking about Jordan's transformation and was so enthusiastic about his new attitude that Maddy almost felt like her best friend was beginning to develop a crush on Jordan.

But Laina, ever so intuitive, reassured Maddy that she didn't have to worry about that. "I'm just relieved to know that you're not involved with the *old* Jordan Sanders," she told Maddy.

"We're not really involved. . .yet," Maddy felt compelled to explain. "Right now, we're just getting to know each other. But you never know what might happen," she said.

"Knowing you. . .you never know," Laina agreed. "But what was all that he kept saying about your mystery crush?" Laina wanted to know. "Is this some sort of secret you haven't told me?"

Maddy sighed. "No, you know who my mystery crush is,

but Jordan doesn't. And now it's gotten a little out of hand. I just haven't found a good way to tell him." Briefly, she explained the conversation she and Jordan had shared that day after leaving the park. "Now he thinks he's helping me learn to cook to impress some guy, and I'm not really sure how to tell him that I did all this to impress him. The only thing is, I figure if I tell him too soon, he'll be upset with me and he won't want to be even my friend anymore."

Laina was silent for a good while. When she spoke, she said, "You're telling me that the reason you spend all this time with Jordan is because you're enrolled in a sort of. . . wife school with Jordan as your teacher?"

"Basically," Maddy nodded.

"And he's only going along because he thinks that you're doing this for some other guy?"

"That's where I'm not so sure. Sometimes I get the feeling he's a little jealous of the other guy. And sometimes, it's like he doesn't really care."

Laina let out a long sigh. "You are the only person I know who could get into a mess like this."

"Well, what am I going to do to get out of it?" Maddy wanted to know. "I was going to tell him tonight, but you saw how well we get along. What if he gets so confused that he won't give me a chance to totally explain the situation. What if he tells me to stay away from him forever?"

Laina shrugged. "I don't know. I've never heard of anything so odd in my whole life. But I think you're going to have to tell him the truth. And soon."

"You're right. I'll call him in a couple of days and set up a time to see him. Then I'll tell him."

ða.

Jordan wearily tugged on Hancock's leash. Although he liked being able to keep his dog with him, instead of at his parents' home, the daily walks were beginning to become somewhat of a chore. Actually, it wasn't the walk itself. Both he and Hancock enjoyed that part. The hard part was trying to get

Hancock to go back home. The dog seemed to have an inner sense about when Jordan decided it was time to head back to the apartment. He would suddenly get extremely stubborn and try to pull Jordan in the opposite direction. The past couple of evenings, Jordan had practically dragged the puppy back to the apartment.

The few people who had happened to witness the tug-of-war had tsk-tsked and pointedly informed Jordan that people like him shouldn't be allowed to own pets if they were going to mistreat them. Jordan had tried to explain that he wasn't trying to hurt the dog, but they had refused to listen. One man had gone so far as to threaten to call the Humane Society to report him.

Today, Jordan had decided to take an easier route. Instead of trying to drag an unwilling puppy home, Jordan had simply picked the puppy up and carried him home, rather than risk an embarrassing scene. Unfortunately, the puppy had proven to be much heavier than he looked. By the time Jordan reached his building, he was grateful that the building had an elevator.

As soon as Jordan opened the apartment door, Hancock ran over to the couch to claim his favorite seat. Jordan followed suit and wearily closed his eyes, still huffing and puffing from the exertion of carrying Hancock. A few seconds later, Hancock moved over and began licking Jordan's face. Jordan petted the puppy for a few minutes before starting dinner.

A few moments after he began looking through the refrigerator for inspiration, the phone rang.

"Hello?" Jordan questioned.

"Hello, Jordan, it's Maddy," was the cheery response on the other line.

"Oh, hi. What's up?"

"Not much. I was sitting here in the kitchen looking at the recipe for the focaccia we started last week, and I decided to finish it myself."

"So how did it turn out?"

"I'll let you know when I take it out of the oven."

"You'll have to save me a piece," Jordan said. He closed the refrigerator and sat down on one of the stools he kept at the kitchen island. "So how's work?"

"Pretty good. The students are really into their internships right now, so they're pretty interested in what I have to say in my classes. They take what they learn in the classes back to their jobs."

"How's your problem student?"

"Not too bad. She's still pretty withdrawn, but she's not causing any problems. In fact, she actually asked me about the Bible today after classes."

Jordan was quiet, unsure of what to say.

"I know I told you I wouldn't get involved," Maddy said, "but how can I refuse to share the gospel with someone? The last time I mentioned Jesus, she ran away, but now that she's asked again—without me forcing it on her, I can't ignore her."

Jordan exhaled loudly, then asked, "What did she want to know?"

"Well, several weeks ago, I told her that Jesus loves her, no matter how other people are treating her. She got upset and said that I didn't understand. That was when she started avoiding me."

"So what did you tell her today?"

"I told her that Jesus does love her. I invited her to come to church with me."

"You what?"

"I invited her to come to church with me."

Jordan closed his eyes. "Maddy, don't you think you're hiding behind rose-colored glasses here?"

"About what?"

"About. . .this." Jordan's words came out in a rush. "I know she needs to hear the gospel, but don't you think you're getting her hopes up a little?"

"How would I be doing that?"

"You know how kids can be. What if she goes to church with you, gets saved, and goes back to class and finds out the kids still don't like her? Aren't you just a little bit worried that she might take it out on you?"

Maddy's voice sparked with indignation. "No, I'm not. The Bible tells us to share the message of salvation with others. When we do that, we run the risk of people being upset with us. But I feel like the Lord allowed me to get this job, and I'm not going to be ashamed of Him, just because you think things won't work out with Trina."

"Maddy, you're right, we have to share the gospel with people, but we have to be careful about how we approach them. Just use common sense."

Maddy was silent for a moment, then she spoke up angrily. "What makes you the expert? You were no saint yourself, but somehow you managed to get saved. I'm assuming someone shared the gospel with you while you were at college. And judging from the way you used to act toward Christians, I doubt you were very receptive at first. Am I right?"

Jordan had to tell the truth. "Right," he said quietly. The memory of how he'd taunted anyone religious burned in his mind as he listened to Maddy.

Maddy seemed to understand his discomfort. When she spoke again, she was more compassionate. "But what if no one ever said anything to you because they were scared of how you might treat them?" she questioned.

Maddy was right. No matter how many times he had teased Christians, they still seemed to always pop up, handing out tracts and inviting him to church. And thanks to them, he knew where to turn when he was ready to make a change. But what about people like Harper Blackston? Where did they fit in? What about Pastor Maneskroll?

Jordan wiped his forehead, and took several deep breaths. It was time to tell Maddy the whole story behind his conversion. "Maddy, I need to talk to you. In person. Can I come over?"

"Jordan, I'm sorry I upset you. But I'll be okay. You don't

need to come over and give me a speech." Her voice was kind, but firm.

"It's important." He was pleading, but he wasn't ashamed. He needed to get this off his chest.

"Oh, all right. But don't try to change my mind about inviting her to church, because I already asked her. She's going to call me on Saturday to let me know if she's coming."

"I'll be there in half an hour." Jordan hung up the phone and left the apartment.

In the car, he tried to concentrate on the road and prayed, "Please let me say the right words to Maddy, Lord. Please keep her safe. And please help this girl Trina by bringing her to You without causing any harm to come to anyone else."

twelve

Maddy heard Jordan's car pull up just as she finished straining a pot of tea. She didn't know why she was making hot tea in the middle of July, but Jordan had sounded so stressed on the phone that she figured a cup of herbal tea might help him feel better.

When the doorbell rang, her dad said, "I'll get it."

From the kitchen, she heard her dad greet Jordan. "Haven't seen you around here for a while. How's the new place?"

"It's coming along."

"I heard Maddy and Laina gave you a hand with painting. Did they give you any help or did you have to spend the whole time cleaning up after them?" her dad asked as he and Jordan entered the kitchen. He winked at Maddy, so she knew he was just kidding with her.

"Dad, please." She smiled. "Of course we helped him. Didn't we, Jordan?"

Jordan's smile was strained, but his eyes sparkled as he added, "I was pretty worried about my floor at first, but it came out looking no worse for the wear."

"That's good," said her dad. "So what's on the menu for tonight? Maddy already made some kind of fancy bread for us."

"Focaccia, Dad," she reminded him.

Jordan shook his head. "No cooking for me today. I just came over to talk."

Maddy's dad eyed Jordan closely. "You okay, son?"

Jordan shrugged. "I think so."

Her dad opened his mouth, then closed it. "I'll be upstairs with Berniece. If you need anything, just let me know." He patted Jordan on the back and headed upstairs.

Jordan stood in the middle of the kitchen with his hands in his pockets. Maddy's heart went out to him. She could tell that whatever was upsetting him was serious. She was glad she hadn't refused to let him come over. But she was at a loss for what to say to comfort him. "Would you like some tea?" she asked, gesturing toward the teapot.

"Sure," he answered.

While she poured the tea, Jordan sat at the kitchen table, silent.

A few minutes later, Maddy joined him. She sat quietly, waiting for him to start talking.

He gazed up from his teacup and looked her in the eye for a moment. "Maddy, only a few people know about this. It's just such a terrible thing. . .I haven't even told anyone at my church."

Maddy's heart started beating wildly. Suddenly, she was uncomfortable with the idea of Jordan confiding anything this serious in her. She reached out and put her hand on top of his. "Then you don't need to tell me. If it's really upsetting you, I can just pray for you."

Jordan hesitated for a moment, as if he were about to agree with her. Then he shook his head, gently pulling his hand away. "No. I need to tell you." He took a deep breath, then began. "When I went away to college, I was the same Jordan you used to know. I wasn't mean, but I teased people—a lot. You know how I was, and you know how the things I said hurt."

Maddy nodded, saying nothing. The way he'd treated her was obviously still bothering him, and she didn't want to add to his trouble by saying too much.

"Well, I acted the same way at college. I was popular, and I teased anybody who seemed. . .I don't know." He shrugged, apparently looking for the right words. "Anyway, there was this guy, Harper Blackston. He was pretty quiet. Really smart. And even back then, I knew he was a brilliant artist. Maybe I was even a little jealous of him. I felt insecure around him, because I knew he was better than me at the time. But he was kind of eccentric, just small things, mostly, so I would try to make myself feel better by teasing him. I wasn't the only one who made fun of him—lots of people did—but I did more than my share. He lived in a dorm room across from mine for the first three years."

Jordan sipped his tea. "Whatever anybody said never seemed to bother him. He just ignored us. He made good grades. He didn't really hang out with a lot of people, so we figured he had friends somewhere else. And the fact that he didn't seem to get upset when we teased him. . .I think it just egged us on. We kept jabbing and digging, just to see what it would take to make him get mad. We thought he was some kind of robot or something. . .he never really paid much attention to us. I wasn't a Christian then, and I know I said some pretty rough stuff, so bad I can't even repeat it now."

Jordan's eyes suddenly grew watery. Looking into his cup, he said, "There was this preacher. His name was Malcolm Maneskroll. He wasn't too much older than all of us, just in his early thirties. He really had a heart for college students."

He looked Maddy in the eye now. "You were a Christian when you went to college, so you probably saw all the bad stuff that went on, but had the sense to stay away from it."

Maddy nodded slightly. She'd made her share of mistakes, but Jordan was right. The support she had from her parents and her church had helped her to steer clear of much of what went on.

Jordan shook his head. "Well, I didn't. But it seemed like this preacher was always popping up somewhere. It was a small college town, and he would stand on the corners in the party district of town, if you could call it that. He would hand out tracts and invite us to his church. I went probably once or twice during my first three years there, and all I did was make fun of him."

Jordan got really quiet and held his head in his hands. Maddy moved closer and patted his back. She had never, ever seen him cry, and she didn't know what she could do to help him. Maddy was a little scared and didn't know if she wanted to hear the rest of the story.

Abruptly, Jordan sat up straight.

"Jordan, you don't have to tell me this."

"Yes," he said. Wiping his eyes with the back of his hands, he started again. "By the time my senior year started, this pastor, Malcolm, had led several students to Christ. And he was working on several others. The college-aged members of his congregation would go out with him and help hand out tracts and witness to people in broad daylight, in the middle of the street. They were really excited about the Lord." Jordan smiled slightly, as though he was recalling a happy memory.

"One of the people he was helping was Harper Blackston. Most of us didn't know it, but the summer before our senior year started, Harper had tried to commit suicide. Not many of the students lived there year-round, but Harper had lived there all his life. His father had died before he was born, and his mother had raised him. She was an alcoholic and a drug addict and had been sentenced to two years in prison for drug abuse, but none of us knew that either. Anyway, Harper called Malcolm after he took all the pills, and Malcolm took him to the hospital. When Harper got better, Malcolm started witnessing to him. Harper wouldn't go to church, though. He was too embarrassed to go, because even some of the people at the church still made fun of him sometimes. But Malcolm was persistent. He invited Harper to his house and let him meet his wife. Harper apparently felt comfortable with them, and he started spending a lot of time there.

"One day, right after Christmas break ended, I was walking downtown to go to the store, and I saw Malcolm. It was early in the morning, and hardly anybody else was out on the street. He stopped me, and he said, 'Jordan, Jesus is waiting for you to make up your mind.' I laughed at him, like I normally did. I told him that since he was always telling us that Jesus was going to be around for eternity, that Jesus could wait another day for me. Then he grabbed my arm, and he got really serious. He said, 'Jordan, if you died today, give me one reason why Jesus shouldn't let you go to hell?'

"I don't know what it was, but I finally listened to him. I think he scared me. Nobody had ever put it to me like that before. We sat down on a park bench, and he read me these Bible verses. He asked me if I believed Jesus was the Son of God. I said yes. Even though I didn't know exactly why I was saying yes, I knew in my heart that Jesus was God's Son, and I knew He had died on the cross for me. Even though I had never thought much about it before, I also knew that Jesus had risen from the dead and was back up in Heaven. But then I thought about some of the things I'd done.

"I told Malcolm, 'I've done some pretty bad things. I don't think God will really forgive some of the stuff I've done.' He told me that Jesus would wash my sins away, and give me a clean slate. He read Romans 8:1 to me and I just felt so relieved. That sounded good to me, and even though I had my doubts, I went ahead and prayed this prayer with him. When we finished, he hugged me and said, 'Welcome to God's family.' He told me I needed to come to church and make a public profession of my faith. I told him no at first, but he just smiled and said, 'I'll see you Sunday.' ·

"The rest of the morning I felt like I was floating on air. I was smiling so much, I felt like my face was going to get stuck. People kept asking me what was making me so happy, and I just kept saying 'Jesus loves me.' A lot of people thought I was making fun of the Christians on campus because they were always saying stuff like that.

"I didn't care what they thought about me, and I didn't try to explain it to anyone. I knew I was feeling better than I had in a long time, and I wasn't making fun of somebody to make me feel happy. My roommate was a Christian, and I remember locking myself in the room later that day and borrowing his Bible. I kept reading those same verses Malcolm had shown me, trying to make sure he was telling me the truth. When my roommate came up after dinner, I started asking him all these questions. I had hardly talked to the guy since he'd gotten saved, but Malcolm had already told him I'd gotten saved, and he was just as excited as I was. He suggested we go out and celebrate at this coffee shop where he was supposed to be meeting Malcolm and some of the other students for a Bible study.

"We left the dorm, and right outside we saw Harper. I wanted to apologize to him, but all I could think to say was, 'Hey, Harper, Jesus loves you.'

"He had never, in three years, said hardly anything to me when I had teased him, but just then, he pushed me up against a concrete wall. He was a big guy, and he could have beat me up any day, but I never realized it until then. I was scared because he was choking me.

"He said, 'Are you telling me Jesus loves you, too?'

"I barely whispered 'yes' before he let me go and just gave me another shove. I had a small cut on the back of my head, where he pushed me against the wall, but I didn't even notice it until later. 'Don't give me that,' he said. He took off running in the other direction. My roommate was pretty shaken up too, and by the time we got to the coffee shop, he asked everybody to pray for Harper.

"Malcolm wasn't there yet, so they just started praying for Harper. They seemed to know he had been going through a rough time, and even though he got along with Malcolm pretty well, he was leery of the rest of them.

"They were all happy that I'd gotten saved, and they told me that they had been praying for me for a long time. I was shocked that they even cared about me that much, since I'd never been that friendly to any of them."

Jordan stopped and cleared his throat. "Malcolm never showed up that night." He looked at over at Maddy. "Do you recognize this story yet?"

Maddy's stomach started flip-flopping. Something about Jordan's story was making her uneasy. The names he'd mentioned seemed familiar. Then, she remembered something from the news a few years ago. She remembered Stacy mentioning that Jordan had attended art school in New Jersey. But somehow, she never connected his name to that school. . . or that story.

She impulsively hugged Jordan. "Oh, Jordan, I'm sorry. I never knew you—I'm sorry." Maddy tried to stop herself, but she started sobbing. Not long after, Jordan was crying along with her. Minutes later, he pulled away.

"An hour later, we left the coffee shop and walked to Malcolm's house."

Maddy held up her hand. "I don't know why you're telling me this, but you don't have to. I know."

He shook his head and continued. Tears were still streaming down his face. "There were police cars everywhere."

Maddy closed her eyes. This much she knew from the news. Harper Blackston had killed Malcolm, and then himself. Malcolm's wife had hid in the bedroom, and later escaped through the back door.

Jordan was still talking. ". . .Malcolm's wife said Harper had been upset because of what I'd said. He didn't believe that Jesus could love me *and* him. It was my fault."

Maddy was silent. She knew Jordan blamed himself, and she could understand why. But surely, he hadn't been carrying this around for all this time?

"I went to Malcolm's funeral. It was on a Sunday. I didn't want to go, but I remembered how Malcolm had wanted me to come to church that Sunday. I just felt like I couldn't let him down. The other students tried to be nice to me, and even though no one ever came right out and said it, most of them blamed me. I thought they had a right to. I never made my profession of faith in Malcolm's church. In fact, I never went back after his funeral. My roommate avoided me whenever it was possible, and even the non-Christians avoided me. The police took me in for questioning, and I couldn't think of anything except how I was responsible."

"Jordan," Maddy said gently. "The news reports. . .most of

the students I saw who were interviewed said they felt responsible. They said everybody teased him. They all said they felt bad."

Jordan shook his head. "I know. But I shouldn't have said anything to him that night. He was upset about me."

"Jordan, he was on medication. He'd tried to commit suicide at least two other times. His doctors said he was unstable."

"Maybe. But maybe not. We'll never know."

"So what happened to you?" Maddy's question was barely above a whisper.

"I couldn't think. I wanted some help. I felt like I had canceled out my salvation, but none of the students who went to the church would give me the time of day. I stopped going to class. The school threatened to kick me out. My dad threatened to sue the school. He was just embarrassed that his son had anything to do with that situation.

"Finally, one day, I was packing up to go home. I didn't know what I was going to do, but I couldn't stay there. My roommate came in with Malcolm's wife. I started crying and begged her to forgive me. She said it wasn't my fault. She said that Harper would get into yelling sessions with Malcolm about other students who laughed at him, even the ones in Malcolm's church.

"The only thing that had been different that time was that Harper had brought a gun. She told me that I was welcome to come to the church, but I refused. I felt too guilty. She gave me one of Malcolm's Bibles. I told her I couldn't take it, but she told me that he had already set it aside to give to me that morning after I'd prayed with him.

"It was an old, worn Bible, and she flipped to Isaiah 43:25 and told me that God had already forgiven me, but as long as I blamed myself, I wouldn't *feel* truly forgiven. She told me that she even struggled with her own guilt concerning Malcolm. She'd felt that she might have been able to prevent it if she had not allowed Malcolm to invite Harper to their home in the first place. Then she gave me the card of this guy who was a

Christian counselor and I called him. I started meeting with him, and he helped me understand God had forgiven me. I was able to stay at school and finish my degree.

"My dad hated the fact that I needed counseling, and even more, he couldn't understand why I wanted a Christian counselor. He blames the school for me becoming a Christian. He thinks they should have put Harper out of school before he did so much harm." Jordan smiled slowly. "We still don't see eye to eye. He hates it when I talk about Jesus. Right before I graduated from art school, I talked him into taking half of the money out of this trust fund he had for me. I wasn't supposed to get the money until after I finished college, but I told him that if he wouldn't take the money out, I would when I was able. I gave it to a fund that Malcolm's wife started for kids who wanted to go to Bible college. My dad was furious. He thinks the counselor brainwashed me into giving my money away. He keeps saying that the Bible turned me into mush." Jordan smiled again, then said, "Basically, he thinks Jesus stole some of his money. Every once in a while, he gets really heated up about it."

"What about your mom?" Maddy asked.

"She's not into religion, but she's glad I found something to help me feel better. She just doesn't want to say anything to set my dad off. So as long as I keep quiet about Jesus, things are okay at their house."

Maddy sighed sympathetically. She couldn't imagine what Jordan had gone through, but even more importantly, she couldn't imagine not being supported by her own parents in her decision to be a Christian. They had set the example for her, and when she was four years old, she had made the decision to accept Jesus for herself.

"Jordan, I'm so sorry," she said again. "Are you okay?"

He gave her a half smile. "Most of the time. Sometimes, I get bogged down with guilt, and it takes me a little while to recover. Being around you is sometimes hard, because of how I used to treat you. But I had to tell someone. Only the people I went to school with, my parents, and my counselor know about this. I haven't told anyone here. Not even the people at my church."

Maddy didn't know what to say. While she was still pondering all that he'd said, Jordan spoke up again. This time, his face grew intense and he held her hand as he spoke.

"Maddy, to be honest with you, I admire you wanting to witness to that girl in your class, but I had to tell you this to make sure you understand the seriousness of something like that. When people have been hurt, you never know exactly how they might react, even to people who genuinely care about them." He looked away for a second. "The three years I've been saved, I've never been able to witness to anyone. I've been too scared. I know it's wrong, but I walk in the other direction. I'm glad you're not afraid to, and I'm even a little jealous. I feel like a coward. I'm a grown man, over six feet tall, and you're more that a foot shorter than me, yet, you have more courage than I do. I witnessed to one person, and look what happened after I did."

Maddy was still shaken. She could understand Jordan's fear. In his happiness over getting saved, he'd told Harper that Jesus loved him, and it had been taken the wrong way.

"That's why I started painting murals," Jordan went on. "It's my silent way of telling people about Jesus. One day, I'll be able to open my mouth and tell people, but until then, this is what I can do."

Maddy nodded. "I don't know what to say. I know it took a lot for you to tell me all of this, and I appreciate it." Nervously, she added, "But I still think I need to invite Trina to church. And I'm sorry about what I said about someone having to witness to you. I didn't know the whole story. But if Malcolm hadn't stopped you that morning, where would you be now?" she asked gently.

Jordan shook his head. "I've asked myself that question a million times. I'm glad he stopped me, but if he hadn't, he might still be alive today. . .or maybe not."

Jordan stood up. "I've kept you up too late. I'd better go."

Maddy stood up and followed him to the door. "Thanks for trusting me enough to share your story. I really appreciate it. Is there anything I can do?"

Jordan smiled. "I can always use prayer. I'm not perfect yet."

Maddy bit her lip, unsure of how to phrase her next question. "Will you be upset with me if I still talk to Trina?"

Jordan exhaled loudly. He looked down at the floor for a long time, then said, "No, I won't. I know that you'll do what the Lord tells you to do. Sometimes I just feel like I need to protect you from what could happen, even though I might be wrong. As long as you follow the Lord's leading, you'll be doing the right thing, I think. The more I think about it, the more I know that Malcolm stopped me just in time." He reached out and enveloped Maddy in a hug.

Maddy leaned against his chest, listening to his heartbeat. She knew Jordan didn't see this as a romantic hug, but just for a moment, she let herself believe that he was hugging her because his love for her was deeper than just friendship. Reluctantly, she pulled away.

Looking him in the eye, she said, "I will pray for you, Jordan. I promise."

"Thanks, Maddy. You don't know how much I appreciate it." Slowly, he opened the door and walked outside. Right before he got into his car, he turned and smiled. "See you later."

Maddy waved as his car disappeared down the street.

thirteen

The next day at school, Maddy felt jumpy. On Thursdays, she taught the juniors, so she didn't expect to see Trina, but nonetheless, no matter how brave she'd tried to be for Jordan, his story had shaken her.

Was Trina someone to be afraid of? Maddy couldn't tell. She tried to not be afraid, but with little success. By the time classes were over, Maddy practically flew out of the building. Her heart pounded as she walked to her car, and only when she was out of the parking lot did her pulse slow back to its normal rate.

When she got home, she found her mother in the kitchen and poured out the whole story that Jordan had told her the night before.

When Maddy finished, she asked her mother, "Do you think I did the wrong thing by inviting Trina to church?"

Berniece Thompson was quiet for a long time. She stared at her hands, deep in thought. Finally, she said, "We raised you and your sister not to be ashamed of your faith. Both of you witnessed to your friends all throughout school, and your dad and I are proud of you. Earlier this summer, when you first started telling us about Trina, I was happy that you were trying to reach out to a student in need."

She paused, and looked Maddy in the eye. "I can't say that Jordan's story hasn't scared me. But not every situation turns out like that. What we can do is pray about this. The Lord will show us what His will is for her, and whether or not He wants you to get personally involved. I do know that even if we don't say anything directly to certain individuals, we can always pray for them. And sometimes, prayer is the route God wants us to take. Other times, He wants us to be more vocal. Why don't we pray about it right now?"

Maddy murmured her agreement. She and her mom bowed their heads right then and asked God for guidance about Maddy's role with Trina.

When they finished, Maddy said, "She said she would call me tomorrow if she was going to come to church. What should I say if she calls?"

"If she wants to come, I think she should," her mother said slowly.

"I feel the same way, too," Maddy agreed. "I guess we'll just have to wait and see what happens."

෧

Later that evening, Maddy went bowling with some of her friends from church. "Did you tell Jordan that you have a crush on him?" Laina asked.

Maddy slapped her hand to her forehead. "Oh, no. I totally forgot."

Laina gave her an I-don't-believe-you stare.

Maddy returned the look. "Trust me, Laina. I saw Jordan yesterday, and I really did forget.

"You can't expect to build a relationship on lies," Laina countered.

Maddy sighed in exasperation. "I know. But. . .I really don't think there is any hope for a relationship anymore."

Laina frowned. "Why not?"

"I can't tell you all of the details, but when he came over last night, he told me some things. I really did forget to tell him about my crush on him, and I'm glad I did, because it wouldn't have been the right time. And now I don't think I need to."

"You're not making any sense."

"I know. What I'm trying to say is, Jordan has changed, but he really is being my friend because he feels so awful about how he used to treat me. I think he's satisfied to keep things the way they are, and I'm not going to push things further by telling him I've liked him all these years. This whole summer, I don't think he's even briefly considered more than a friendship with me."

"Are you sure?"

"Almost one hundred percent positive. To Jordan, being my friend is sort of a step of faith. A test to see if I would really forgive him for how he treated me. And all I can say is I'm glad I accepted his apology. I think it would have hurt him if I hadn't."

"So that's it?" Laina asked.

"Yeah."

"But wait—doesn't he think you have a crush on some other guy?"

Maddy shrugged. "Maybe. But I never did. I had the crush on him. When I see him, I'll tell him the crush is over."

"Is it really?"

"I think so. I still care for Jordan, but I can't tell what's real, mature love from my old schoolgirl crush, or just wanting to help him with what he's going through. Now is not the time to cloud things up by being impulsive."

Laina's eyes softened. "You know what I think?"

"What?"

"I think that you're on the right track. You can't make a decision like that based on how you feel from day to day. Like Arnold and Patty are always telling us, lasting love is based on what you know, not what you feel."

"Yeah, good old Arnold and Patty," said Maddy. "I wish Jordan could meet Arnold. I think they'd get along pretty well. Unfortunately, Jordan seems to get really upset when I mention Arnold. I can't figure it out."

Laina laughed. "Maybe he thinks Arnold is your mystery crush," she said, wiggling her eyebrows.

"Oh, right." Maddy laughed. "Jordan is jealous of the married man who leads the singles' group with his wife?"

"You did tell him Arnold is married, didn't you?"

"Yes. . .well, I think I did." Maddy grew silent as she thought back to the day she and Jordan had taken Hancock to the park. That was the first day she'd ever mentioned Arnold. She couldn't remember whether or not she'd told Jordan that Arnold was married. Then her mind flashed back to the day of Jordan's apology. She'd been so rude, trying to get away from him and—"Oh, no! The guy on the telephone," she groaned.

"What guy?" asked Laina.

Maddy swallowed. "It's a long story, but the first time Jordan tried to apologize to me, I got scared. I thought he was going to start teasing me. He was standing at the front door, asking to come in, but I wanted him to go away. The phone rang and it was this guy selling long distance services. His name was Arnold, and I played like I knew him. I exaggerated a little, and Jordan must have thought that I had a crush on some guy named Arnold. And then whenever I mentioned Arnold from church, Jordan got really tense. Especially when I told him we were planning a surprise party for Arnold." Maddy covered her face with her hands. "I can't believe I didn't put the two together all this time."

"Me, either," said Laina. "How could you not remember?"

Maddy tried to remember. "A lot happened that day. By the time I saw Jordan again, he was apologizing, and I totally forgot about my little telephone episode."

"Yikes," Laina said. "I'd say you should tell him the next time you see him. You can't have him walking around, mad at Arnold any longer."

"You're right. But for other reasons, I don't want to burden him by telling him I had a crush on him. He has a lot to think about now."

"Do what you have to," said Laina. "But just get it done."

❧

The next morning, Maddy awoke to the sound of the phone ringing. Groggily, she leaned over and picked up the phone. It was probably Trina.

"Hello?" she said.

"Hi, it's Jordan."

Maddy sat up. "Hi."

"Are you busy today?"

"I don't know. I figured I'd wait around for a while in case Trina calls, but my parents should be here if she does. What did you have in mind?"

"Do you want to ride out to Powell Gardens with me?"

Maddy thought for a moment. Today would be a good day to talk to Jordan. "Sure. What time? I'd prefer to leave in the afternoon sometime, if you don't mind."

"How's two o'clock?"

"Two is fine. I'll see you later."

During the morning, Maddy did a little housecleaning. By noon, she was done and she restlessly sat waiting for Trina to call. While she waited, she got out her Bible and began to pray. At first, her prayers were about Trina. As time went on, her prayers shifted to Jordan.

Lord, please show me what to say to Jordan. I don't think now is a good time to tell him about my crush on him, but I want to be honest. Is he the husband You've chosen for me? And if he isn't, how should I treat him? I hate to pull away from him right now, after everything he's told me, but I don't want to keep going, not knowing what he's feeling. I don't want either of us to get hurt, but right now, I feel more scared for myself than for Jordan. I think I care about him way more than he does for me. Please show us both Your will. In Jesus' name, Amen.

Maddy opened her eyes and wiped away tears. It was in the Lord's hands now.

Jordan came at exactly two o'clock. Maddy was outside, talking to Mrs. Myston when he pulled up.

"Where's that dog of yours, Jordan?" Mrs. Myston asked, looking around suspiciously.

Jordan put his hands out in front of him. "I had to leave him at home. You can't take pets to Powell Gardens."

"Oh. Powell Gardens is such a pretty place. Be sure and stop by the chapel. It's beautiful." She smiled.

"Are you ready?" he asked Maddy.

"Sure. Let's go. Good-bye, Mrs. Myston," she said, waving to the woman.

"Take care, you two," she returned.

"We will," said Jordan.

In the car, Maddy decided it was a good time to get her confession out. Powell Gardens was a good forty-five minute drive out Highway 50 in Kingsville, Missouri.

"Ahem. I have something to tell you," she told Jordan, after they'd been riding for almost ten minutes.

"I have something to tell you, too," he grinned, looking across at her.

"Oh? Who goes first, then?" she asked.

"You. I'll tell you later on."

"Okay. Well. First off. . .I think we have had a miscommunication." Maddy went on to tell Jordan the story of the two Arnolds, and how she didn't have a crush on either of them.

"I see," Jordan said. "So I was all worked up over the wrong guy."

"And about the mystery crush," Maddy went on. "It's over. I was never really clear about my feelings for the guy, so. . .I put it all in God's hands for now. I'm not going to worry about it anymore."

Jordan just nodded. "So you're not going to tell me who he is?"

Maddy shook her head. "I don't think it's all that important right now."

"I see," he said. Abruptly, he changed the subject. "So did Trina call you today?"

Maddy shook her head. "She may call later on, though."

"Yeah," said Jordan.

Silence enveloped them for a few minutes before Maddy decided to strike up another conversation. "So how's Hancock doing? Is he still refusing to come home after his walks?"

Jordan laughed. "Yeah. And he's getting way too heavy to carry. I enrolled him in obedience school. He starts in two weeks."

"Good idea," Maddy said.

Once again, the conversation lulled, but this time, neither of them made any attempt to restart it. The rest of the ride was continued in silence.

When they reached Powell Gardens, the parking lot was crowded. Apparently, lots of people had decided to come out to enjoy the place.

Maddy and Jordan entered through the visitors' center, paid the admission fee, then stepped outside, where the garden walkways began.

"Which way do you want to go?" asked Jordan. "The rock and waterfall garden or the chapel first?"

Maddy glanced at the small map she'd picked up inside. It had been years since she'd been to Powell Gardens. She remembered the place was big. It spanned over eight hundred acres and had been originally purchased by George Powell, Sr. Later, it was used as a dairy farm, a Boy Scout camp, and a natural resource center before it was converted to a botanical garden open to the public in 1988.

"How about we walk to the perennial garden, by way of the rock and waterfall garden? Then we could work our way to the chapel and see the wildflower meadow on the way," Maddy suggested.

"Good idea," Jordan agreed.

As they walked, they were quiet, content to watch others enjoying the garden. Many families had come out, and it was amusing to watch toddlers and little kids stopping and examining everything that was growing, even down to blades of grass.

After they crossed the bridge from the island in the middle of the lake, they headed to the rock gardens. They spent quite some time walking through the shaded garden, enjoying hydrangeas, dogwoods, and other shade-loving flowers and shrubs. "I hear that it's really beautiful in the spring when all the azaleas are in bloom," Jordan told her.

"I bet it's gorgeous," Maddy said. "Listen to the sound of the water. Isn't it peaceful?"

"It is."

They shared an amiable silence as they walked through the perennial gardens, which were aglow with color. This garden was actually a series of different gardens, ranging from woodland gardens, a secret garden, a butterfly garden, and prairie gardens, in addition to a garden of flowers familiar to the Kansas City area.

As they headed past the wildflower meadow to the chapel, Jordan joked, "Have you seen enough flowers yet?"

"I think so." Maddy laughed. "It's all starting to blur together. What was your favorite?"

"I liked the butterfly garden, actually," said Jordan.

"I did, too," said Maddy. "But I think my favorite was the fragrance garden."

"That was nice, too."

A few moments later, a family came from the opposite direction on the path. Three children walked a few feet ahead of their parents. The two older boys, probably around six or seven years old, were laughing and giggling. Just behind them was a darling little girl who looked to be about two years old. Smiling shyly, when she passed by Maddy and Jordan, she paused for a moment, looked up into their faces and shyly said, "Hi."

Maddy and Jordan stopped and said hello to the girl and her parents who were a few feet away.

"She was adorable," Maddy said after the family had passed.

"I know. It's amazing how little kids are so trusting. They'll stop and talk to complete strangers and not even be afraid."

"I know. Look, there's the chapel," said Maddy. She began to walk at a quicker pace until Jordan stopped her.

"Hey, slow down. I'm too tired to go that fast. We've been walking for miles."

Maddy closed her eyes, then opened them. "Miles?"

Jordan pulled out his map of the grounds. "According to this map, by the time we finish touring all of the attractions, we will have walked over a mile and a half. In case you haven't noticed, it's pretty hot out here. I'm trying to conserve energy."

"Okay, I'll slow down," Maddy apologized. Jordan was right. It was pretty warm out.

As they walked, she concentrated on the chapel which was getting closer with every step they took. The chapel was a small, angular structure that sat at the far edge of the lake, bordered by woodlands on one side. The other sides were bordered with water, an extension of the wildflower meadow, and natural grasses.

Part of her rush to get to the chapel was wanting to find out what Jordan had to tell her. He had said he would tell her when they reached the chapel, and her curiosity was getting the better of her. *Be patient,* she reminded herself.

Jordan's steps seemed to be agonizingly slow, but Maddy had a feeling he was carefully considering what he wanted to say, so she didn't rush him.

Surprisingly, no one was in the chapel when they got there. Once they were inside, Maddy forgot her impatience. The wood bracing that comprised the walls cast diamond-shaped patterns and shadows all around them. Although it was man-made, the structure blended well in its natural setting. It was simplistic, but beautiful. Maddy sat on one of the benches, just staring at the elaborate patterns of surrounding timber.

It was noisy, but quietly so, with the sound of the wind and birds echoing through the small room.

Jordan sat down next to her. She heard him take a deep breath, and she knew the time had come for what he wanted to share.

Maddy looked him in the eye, and saw an intensity and determination that she hadn't ever seen in him. She braced herself for what might be coming.

Jordan began without pomp or ceremony. "The other night, after I left your house, I couldn't sleep, thinking about Malcolm and everything that had happened. I felt like I had left some loose ends there. His wife had written me two or three letters, letting me know what was going on with church, but I never answered them. The next day, I got another one of the letters and decided to give her a call. She told me that the church has really grown, and they were getting close to finishing a larger building. There's a new pastor now, of course, and she recently remarried. This month, they've been putting the finishing touches on the new church, and next week, they're having a service each night to dedicate the new church. She said she'd thought about asking me to come, but she didn't want to upset me. But when I called her, she decided to go ahead and ask. She wanted to know if I'd come and give a small speech one of the nights, since I donated a lot of the money to the church's college fund. She thought I might want to meet some of the students who've benefitted from it."

Maddy closed her eyes in relief. She hadn't known what Jordan was going to say, and not knowing made her nervous. She turned to face him. "Are you going to go?"

He nodded slowly. "I think so. I feel like I need to. I never made a public profession of faith. I feel like the Lord wants me to go."

Maddy nodded understandingly. "Then I think you should go. How long are you going to be there?"

"I thought I'd catch a plane early on Monday and stay until the main service on Sunday morning."

"That's over a week," Maddy said gently. "Do you think you'll be okay?"

He didn't answer at first, but looked toward the front of the chapel, out the big windows that overlooked the water. Finally, he said, "I think I won't be okay if don't go."

"I understand," Maddy said. And she did. It was something he needed to do for himself, and she knew he would feel badly if he didn't do it. Part of her was a little disappointed. She'd all but made it clear that she wasn't dating anyone, and she wasn't interested in anyone. She'd been hoping that now Jordan would ask her out, but his words had put an end to her hopes and sealed her convictions about their relationship. He viewed her as someone to confide in about his past, and it was her duty as a friend to support him as he continued to heal.

"I knew you'd understand. My parents were far from thrilled about it when I told them last night, but I think they'll understand someday."

Maddy just nodded. Apparently, she was less of a confidante than she had thought she was. He'd told his parents before he'd told her. They sat for another ten minutes or so, each of them lost in their own thoughts, until Jordan stood up. "You ready to head back?"

"I guess so."

As they stepped out of the chapel, Jordan took hold of Maddy's hand. She was surprised, but didn't say anything. When they reached the car, he finally let go of her hand.

"Are you hungry?" he asked, once they were on the highway headed home.

Maddy checked her watch. It was nearly six o'clock, but she didn't have an appetite. "Not really," she said apologetically. She figured Jordan was probably pretty hungry.

He looked at her with concern. "You look pretty worn out. I probably shouldn't have kept you out in the sun so long. Do you want me to take you home?"

"I think so. I've got to substitute teach a friend's Sunday school class in the morning," she told him. "And you know how it is with little kids. You can't afford to look tired because they'll pick up on it and get the better of you before you realize it," she joked.

When they reached her house, Jordan walked her inside and made her promise that she would drink lots of liquids, in case she was a little dehydrated.

Maddy laughingly agreed, and she felt touched by his concern. Before he left, he gave her a quick hug, and then said, "Thanks for being so understanding, Maddy. I know I might have seemed a little self-centered today, and I'm sorry you had to put up with my being so quiet. The gardens are such a good place to think, but it was good to have you there with me."

"Don't worry about me," she told him. "I did my own share of thinking today, too."

"So you're not upset with me?" he questioned.

She shook her head. "I guess I'm just starting to feel a little more. . .contemplative myself. Is that a real word?"

"I think so." He laughed. "I'll either call you before I leave or after I get there Monday, depending on what time my flight is."

"Okay, I'll be waiting," she told him.

fourteen

The rest of the weekend passed quietly for Maddy. Monday morning, she waited as long as she could to hear from Jordan before she left for work, but when he didn't call, she assumed his flight had been an early one. As she walked into her class-room, she wondered what she would say to Trina, who had not called on Saturday or come to church with her. To her surprise, Mrs. Calvin was waiting for her.

"Good morning, Ms. Thompson," said the woman.

"Hi, Mrs. Calvin. How was your weekend?"

"Good, and yours?"

"Mine went well," answered Maddy.

"I don't have a lot of time for conversation, Maddy," the woman said. Her forehead was wrinkled with concern. "I'm actually here concerning one of the students."

"Which one?" Maddy asked.

"Trina Sheppard."

"What's happened?" Maddy was instantly alert.

Mrs. Calvin shook her head. "We don't know. Apparently, she's run away from home."

"When?" Maddy breathed.

"Saturday, we think. Her parents are really worried. They figured she'd come home in time for classes, but she didn't. They told me she mentioned you a lot at home, and I knew you tried to help her. They were wondering if you'd heard from her."

Maddy sat down at her desk, feeling deflated. "No, I haven't," she said, shaking her head. "Did they really think she'd contact me?"

"They had hoped so, but I guess she didn't. I'll go call them now."

"Please, let me know if you hear anything," Maddy requested.

The rest of the day went by in a blur. Right before Maddy left for home, she stopped by Mrs. Calvin's office, only to learn that Trina still hadn't contacted her parents.

That evening, Maddy's parents had dinner at her sister's house, but Maddy stayed home in case Trina or Jordan called. While she waited, Maddy prayed for both Jordan and Trina.

At nine thirty, she still hadn't heard from either of them. Refusing to allow herself to worry, Maddy went to the kitchen to make some tea. Just as the water started boiling, the phone rang. Anxiously, Maddy grabbed the phone. "Hello?"

"Hi. It's me, Jordan. Are you okay?"

Maddy relaxed a little. Jordan had finally called. And she was touched to know that he could sense everything wasn't okay.

"I think so," Maddy said hesitantly. She didn't want to subject Jordan to any stress by launching into an explanation of what was going on with Trina.

"Do you want to tell me about it?" he asked.

Maddy shook her head, even though he couldn't see her. "No. But how was your day?"

"It's been pretty rough at times. But I'm glad I'm here. The church has grown so much over the past few years. Most of the congregation came to the prayer service tonight, and I'd say there were at least two hundred and fifty people there."

"Wow," Maddy said.

"The service wasn't really that long. It was just about an hour or so, and it wasn't really structured or scheduled. The pastor just stood at the podium, prayed, and then encouraged everyone to spend a few minutes praying silently on their own. I got down on my knees and before I knew it, the pastor was standing up, praying the closing prayer. It was really special. I feel—I don't know. But I feel better somehow."

"I'm happy for you."

"I saw Malcolm's wife this morning," Jordan said. Maddy

heard the tone of his voice grow more serious. Instead of replying to his statement, she waited for what he would say next.

"She seems really pleased that I decided to participate in the dedication services. I told her that I felt like I had been running from something since I'd left. And even though it was hard to come back, I felt relieved, somehow, to be there."

"Really?"

"Really. I don't know what it is. I also met the new pastor and his wife. After the service, I went to their house and told him my story in a nutshell. He wants me to give my talk at the service on Sunday."

"So you are staying the whole week?" Maddy asked. She was happy for Jordan, but the thought of having to deal with Trina being missing while Jordan was away for a week made her feel alone, even though she knew she could talk to her family or Mrs. Calvin about it. She just didn't want to tell him the bad news over the phone.

"Yeah. And I'm really nervous about it. I wish I could do it tomorrow or something and get it over with. I feel like I might freeze up or start crying in front of all those people."

Maddy's heart melted, knowing that it was very uncharacteristic of Jordan to admit to being afraid of something. Yet, within the space of a week, he had chosen to voice some of his most personal fears and worries to her. She knew she couldn't take his words lightly. "I know you'll do fine. And if you want, I can pray for you."

Maddy could almost see Jordan smile. "That would be great," he said. "I was hoping you'd say that."

"No problem," Maddy answered.

"But that's enough about me. How did things go with Trina today?" Jordan inquired.

"Actually, I didn't see her," Maddy told him. Then, she quickly gave him a brief explanation about what had happened.

Jordan's voice grew more concerned. "I was worried that something like this might happen. I just wish I were there with you."

"Jordan, don't be silly. There's nothing you can do about it now, except pray," Maddy told him, trying to sound more confident than she actually felt.

"I really don't like the way this sounds," Jordan persisted.

"Neither do I, and I'm worried for her." Maddy sighed. "She doesn't seem like the type of kid to just run away, and I don't think she has many friends to turn to. I just hope nothing has happened to her."

"I guess you're right. There's nothing I can do," Jordan said.

"Exactly. Don't worry about me. But do pray for Trina."

"I will. And I'll try to call you back tomorrow or maybe Wednesday. And if you can, would you stop by my parents' house sometime this week and visit Hancock? They're keeping him while I'm gone, but I bet he'd be glad to see you."

"Sure. And I'll let you go since you're calling long distance," Maddy told him. "Talk to you later."

" 'Bye," said Jordan before he hung up.

❧

Tuesday morning, Maddy left for work early and went straight to Mrs. Calvin's office before she went to her own classroom. She could tell by the look on the woman's face that there was either no news or bad news.

"Nothing yet?" Maddy asked disappointedly.

"No. I'm sorry, Maddy," Mrs. Calvin said gently. "But if I hear anything. . ."

"Thanks, Mrs. Calvin, and I won't keep bugging you about this. I'll just keep praying."

Mrs. Calvin nodded soberly. "That might be the best thing."

Maddy left the office with a heavy heart, determined to keep her attitude upbeat and positive for her students' sake.

When she got home after work, Jordan called to tell her he was on his way to the Tuesday evening service. Their conversation lasted less than five minutes.

Maddy helped her mother cook dinner, but started feeling restless soon afterward.

"Didn't you tell Jordan that you would play with his dog?" her mother asked in an attempt to take Maddy's mind off Trina.

"Yeah, I did. I think I'll go over now."

"You could take him to the park or something," her mother suggested.

Maddy nodded in agreement. "I think that would probably be good for both of us. In fact, I'll call Stacy and see if she wants to come."

"Good idea," said her mother.

Twenty minutes later, Maddy was in her car on the way to her sister's house, turning around every two minutes to tell Hancock to stop trying to jump into the front seat. Once, he jumped into the front seat, anyway, landing partially in Maddy's lap. Between trying to drive and getting the exuberant dog into the back seat, Maddy nearly had a fender bender with the rear bumper of the car in front of her at a traffic light. "When I tell Jordan about this, you're going to be in big trouble, buddy," she told him, trying to sound as stern as possible. Hancock didn't seem to mind her warning, but he didn't try to jump in the front again for the rest of the ride. Still, Maddy was a little shaken from the near miss, and by the time they reached Stacy's house, Maddy was relieved.

Getting out of the car, she warned Hancock to stay where he was, and he whimpered in reply. Stacy came out to meet her. Maddy asked, "I think we have a slight change of plans. Would you mind if we played with Hancock in your backyard?"

Stacy glanced at the huge dog in Maddy's backseat. "That's fine. But why are we skipping the park?"

Maddy groaned. "Because I don't think my nerves will last that long." She then told Stacy about Hancock's antics on the way over. "Jordan's putting him in obedience school next week, and it's not a moment too soon."

Maddy got Hancock out of the car and kept a firm hold on his leash while they walked through Stacy's house on their way to the backyard. When they were safely away from anything breakable and within the confines of the small, grassy yard, Maddy let the dog run free. For several minutes, she and Stacy took turns throwing a ball for him to retrieve.

"So tell me how things are with Jordan. Mom told me some of what happened with him at his school. That's pretty tough."

Maddy nodded. "Yeah, he's had a hard time with it. But from what I can tell, he's glad to have the chance to go back."

"That's good," Stacy commented. "But what about you and him? Is there more than a friendship?"

"No." Maddy shook her head.

"Why not? Mom said he spends enough time at the house to be an extra kid. Hasn't he dropped any hints?"

"Maybe. Maybe not. I'm not really sure. Or maybe I don't know how to read hints anymore. For a while, I thought he might be interested when he thought I had a crush on someone else. But when I told him there was no other guy, I think he might have lost interest."

Stacy eyed her incredulously. "You're telling me that all this time you haven't told him you were interested in him?"

Maddy nodded.

"That's not going to get you anywhere," Stacy said.

"I know. The thing was, I was all set to tell him, but first, I had to make sure things were okay between him and Laina. She was still upset with him for the way he used to act. By the time that was settled, I was ready to tell him, but then he told me about the terrible tragedy at his college. All of a sudden, my confession didn't seem that important anymore. And besides, if I told him and he wasn't interested, I'd feel like I was putting undue stress on him when he's already going through so much. He might feel like he has to return my interest, just because I've listened to him and tried to be supportive when he's having such a struggle."

"You're right about that," Stacy agreed.

Both women were silent for a few minutes, while they watched Hancock chase his tail.

Suddenly, Stacy spoke up again. "Would you tell him if you didn't think he'd feel pressured to be more than friends?"

"I'd love to," Maddy confessed. "But I seem to time it wrong."

"I suggest you jump in and just say it the next time you see a safe opening. Otherwise, you're stringing yourself along. He has no idea what you feel about him and vice versa."

"You're right. I don't want to just blurt it out, without any preface. I do stuff like that way too much and it gets me in trouble. Like the day on the telephone with that other Arnold." Maddy sighed and hugged her knees to her chest. "I just wish I could make it more special."

"Like how?"

Maddy shrugged. "I don't know. Like cook him dinner or something—now that I know how to cook," she joked.

Stacy smiled. "I really can't believe he taught you how to cook."

"It wasn't that hard. I don't think it was so much that I couldn't learn. . .I think I was just *ready* to learn."

"You're probably right. But it's still funny that he actually came over and gave you lessons. What a way to get to know the guy you have a crush on." Stacy laughed.

Maddy arched an eyebrow. "Hey, it worked, didn't it?"

"Too bad you didn't have a graduation."

"Yeah, too bad," Maddy agreed. "I don't know what a ceremony for that would be like, though."

"Instead of walking across the stage, you'd just stroll across the kitchen floor," Stacy quipped.

"Yeah, and instead of a diploma, he'd hand me a rolling pin," Maddy laughingly added.

"And instead of one of those long robes, you'd have to wear an apron," said Stacy.

"And a chef's hat!" Maddy added. The two dissolved into giggles at this last image, laughing until their stomachs hurt.

Several minutes later, after they had suppressed most of their laughter, Maddy stood up. "I'd better get Hancock home before it gets too late," she told her sister. "I don't want him jumping into my lap if it's dark outside."

"Well, thanks for coming over. Maybe by the time Jordan gets back, he'll be feeling better so you can tell him."

"Hopefully."

"Maybe you can even have that ceremony."

"Yeah, sure." Maddy smiled. "Or maybe we can have the 'practice' conversation," she joked.

"Practice conversation?" Stacy asked.

"Yeah." Maddy laughed. "Jordan is always bugging me to let him help me figure out what to tell the guy. He wants me to 'practice' the whole conversation on him."

Stacy said nothing, but lifted an eyebrow. "You know," Maddy continued, "come to think of it, he might not have such a bad idea. Sometimes I've wanted to practice the conversation on him, and then end up by telling him that he's the guy." She glanced over at Stacy and laughed. "What do you think? Should I do it? I could even cook him dinner."

Stacy thought for a moment. Finally, she said, "It might be workable. . .although it is a pretty roundabout way of doing it."

"Yeah. He might think I was totally nuts by the time I finished," Maddy said.

"Might?" Stacy laughed.

Maddy gently shoved her sister. "All right, that's enough. I know it's a silly idea. But hey, at this point I'm willing to try it."

"Are you serious?" Stacy asked incredulously.

Maddy stood up. "Actually, I'm really considering it. I can't say for sure, but it's the closest I've come to an actual plan so far."

Stacy shrugged. "Whatever you feel comfortable with. Do you need any help?"

Maddy put her hands on her hips. "Oh, sure. Ms. Wedding Coordinator always wants to plan everyone else's party."

"I do not!" Stacy laughed.

"Yes, you do." Maddy giggled. "But if I decide to do this, I might give you a call—but only for a little advice. I don't want you taking over."

"Just let me know what I can do," Stacy persisted.

"I will. And there is one thing you can do for me right now. Pray for Trina. I hope she's somewhere safe."

Stacy instantly sobered. "I will." She hugged Maddy and said, "I think she's going to be okay, but I'll keep praying."

That night, Maddy tossed and turned as she had the night before. Not only was she concerned about Jordan and Trina, but she kept trying to decide whether or not she should have the dinner for Jordan.

After several hours, Maddy sat up and turned on the lamp next to her bed. It occurred to her that after nearly four months of being in a semi-relationship with Jordan, she was more confused than she'd been in the beginning. Constantly trying to protect her feelings from the pain of rejection had led to a dead end. Stacy was right. It would be better to just get things out in the open. Otherwise, she and Jordan could go on for months and months, maybe even years, not knowing where the other stood.

Lord, should I tell Jordan how I feel about him? Before she could even finish praying, a Bible verse came to her memory. *The truth will set you free.*

"I guess that's Your answer, Lord," she said. Almost instantly, a feeling of peace washed over her. *Now, if only telling Jordan would be so easy.*

Maddy sighed, knowing she would spend the next few days gathering all her courage. But it was time. She valued her friendship with Jordan, but if the Lord didn't want there to be more, she had to do something soon; otherwise, she would be deceiving herself. And there was no escaping the wisdom of God's word. Telling the truth would make her free, whether or not Jordan decided he loved her more than a friend.

fifteen

Wednesday evening, Maddy had just gotten home from work when the phone rang. Hoping it would be Jordan, Maddy ran to the phone. "Hello?"

"Um, Ms. Thompson?" The voice of the girl was familiar.

"Yes," Maddy replied, trying to put a face with the voice.

"This is Trina," the girl said.

"Trina! Where are you? Your parents are so worried about you."

"I know. I'm home now, but Mrs. Calvin asked me to call you after my parents told her I was back."

Maddy remained silent, not knowing what she should say.

"I'm sorry I didn't call you back about going to church," said Trina.

Maddy felt tears of relief coming to her eyes. "That's okay. Just don't run off like that again." Then she added, "And the invitation is still on, if you want to come."

"Well, actually, that's what I wanted to tell you about. I don't want to take up too much of your time, but I wanted to tell you what happened."

"Go ahead, I'm listening." Maddy sat down on the sofa and waited. She heard Trina take a deep breath.

"I didn't mean to run away. I went out Saturday to one of the clubs that some of the kids at my school go to. I met this guy there, and he seemed really interested in me, and he invited me to a party at one of his friends' house. It was really late, but I decided to go anyway. I was just feeling so bad about myself, and I decided that I was going to do whatever I needed to do to make friends. Everyone at the party was older than me; most of the people were in college, so they had drugs and alcohol. I didn't want to get drunk, and

I've never done drugs, so I kept refusing whenever anybody offered me some. The guy who'd invited me started teasing me because I wouldn't, so I decided to leave. But I felt so depressed that I got on the road and just kept driving. I drove most of the night and I just didn't want to go home. On Sunday morning, it seemed like I kept passing by all of these churches, and I kept thinking about how you invited me to go to your church. Finally, I think I was somewhere in the middle of Kansas, and I saw this little church by the side of the road. I don't know why I did it, but I pulled over and sat outside of the window and listened, because I was too ashamed to go inside.

"The preacher was talking about some of the same things you told me about—how Jesus loves us no matter how other people feel about us." Trina stopped talking and Maddy could hear she was sobbing.

"Trina, do you want to call me back and tell me the rest later?" Maddy asked gently. "I'll be home all this evening."

"No. I want to finish telling you. He talked about praying this prayer to ask Jesus to forgive me of my sins and come into my heart, but I didn't feel ready to pray that yet. I got up and walked over to my car. I tried to drive away, but the car wouldn't start. So when everyone came out of the church, I was sitting in the parking lot, with a car that wouldn't go anywhere. The pastor and his wife came over to me and invited me to their house for dinner. I couldn't believe they did that because they didn't even know me, but I felt safe. They told me that the Lord told them to invite me. So I went to their house, and that's where I was until this morning."

"Why didn't you call?" Maddy asked, starting to feel a little angry. "We didn't know if you were safe or not."

Trina sighed. "I don't know. The pastor's wife kept asking me about my family, and I lied and told her I didn't have any family. They reminded me of my grandparents, and I didn't want to explain to them why I had run away, since I wasn't even sure why I'd done it in the first place. They said they didn't believe me, but I could stay with them until I got a job and earned some money to get my car fixed, as long as I went to church with them."

"So then what happened?"

"I stayed there, and they kept asking me if I knew Jesus. I told them I knew about Him, but I still didn't want to pray that prayer. Then Tuesday night, I went to a Bible study with them. This lady stood up and gave a testimony about all of the bad things she had gone through before she finally got saved. I knew then that if I didn't do something, I could end up like she did and maybe worse. So when they asked if anybody wanted to pray the prayer and get things straight with Jesus, I went to the front of the church and prayed."

"Oh, Trina, I'm so happy for you!" Maddy exclaimed.

"Thanks, Ms. Thompson. And I feel happier than I have been in a long time. This morning I told Pastor Walston and his wife that I needed to call home, and my parents drove out to pick me up. Then two other things happened. First, my parents got saved. Then, when my dad tried to start my car, it started perfectly. I think God wanted me there for a reason."

"So where are you going to go to church now?" Maddy asked.

"My parents and I agreed to start going to churches beginning Sunday until we find one we like. And I've decided to stay here my first two years of college instead going away right now. I think my parents and I can get to know each other better now that we're all thinking alike."

"I'm glad. I think you're making a good decision," said Maddy. "So will I see you in class Friday?"

"Well. . .no. I told Mrs. Calvin that I'm quitting the program. There's only about a week and a half left to the camp, and school starts in another couple weeks. I need to get everything in order since I have to apply to a different school this fall. But maybe we'll visit at your church someday."

"I'd like that," said Maddy. "And I understand about your quitting. But thanks for calling to let me know what happened. I've had a lot of people praying for you the past few days."

"Tell them I really appreciate it," Trina said. "And I want to thank you for not giving up on me even when I was being so rude. I'm really sorry, and I didn't mean it, but I know better now."

"I forgive you." Maddy's reply was sincere. "And I'll be praying for you when you start school."

"Thanks. I know it might not be easy to make friends, but just like you said, it's better to be myself and make friends instead of trying to be someone other people want me to be. I don't want to mess up again trying to be someone I'm not. If Jesus can love me, I'm sure I can find some other Christians who'll treat me like you did."

Maddy swallowed. It felt good to know that she had done the right thing. And she was glad the Lord had intervened before things got any worse for Trina. "I'm so happy you feel that way, Trina," Maddy said.

"Me, too. But I've got to get off the phone. My parents need to call some other people and let them know I'm okay. But maybe I can call you sometime?"

"Sure. And if I'm not home, just leave a message and I'll call you back as soon as I can."

"Okay. 'Bye, Ms. Thompson."

"Good-bye, Trina." Maddy hung up the phone and smiled. Apparently, God hadn't wanted Trina to visit her church Sunday. But, judging from the outcome, things couldn't have turned out any better. She was just about to go tell her parents the good news when the phone rang again.

❧

"I should have called sooner," Jordan told himself as he hung up the phone. His conversation with Maddy had left him feeling disabled by mixed emotions. At the time he'd made the call, it had seemed like a good idea, but now, things had seemed to take a turn in a direction that didn't suit his plans.

He'd been both happy and relieved to hear that Trina had returned and was starting to make some changes in her life. Looking back, he felt that he had almost certainly overreacted about Maddy's initial zealousness to reach out to the girl. God had a plan for Trina, and if Maddy hadn't listened to the Lord's leading, things might have ended differently. Or maybe not. Jordan couldn't say for sure. God has a way of getting someone else to do the job if another person refuses, as Jordan's pastor had a habit of saying. But the news about Trina was not what was concerning him at the moment. It was the dinner.

The day had been ideal until Maddy had told him of her latest plan. He'd spent the morning and afternoon walking around, trying to put his feelings into perspective. He'd known almost since the moment he and Maddy had met again that he had feelings for her. As the summer had progressed, Jordan had felt it would be pretty safe to wait and see how things panned out with her mystery crush. And he'd felt certain that his efforts and prayers had been rewarded when Maddy had confessed at the gardens that day that she no longer had any feelings for the guy. Right then and there he'd wanted to drop to his knees and propose to her, but he hadn't because he knew it would be too sudden for her. He couldn't expect her to transfer her feelings over to him at the drop of a hat. And he knew that he needed to come back here to settle his own feelings about his past before he considered a serious relationship. The emotions and fears he'd experienced here had still been very much alive, although hidden beneath his cheerful exterior. But he knew that he needed peace. It would not be fair to carry that type of turmoil into a marriage.

And so far, he was finding a way to put all of the negative memories behind him. He was prepared to forgive himself for good and move on. He'd planned to take Maddy somewhere and tell her all of this as soon as he returned home. She knew what he'd been through, and she understood why he needed to come here. He'd figured that once he explained that he loved her and wanted to spend the rest of his life with her, she'd—

She'd what? Jordan asked himself. He sighed and leaned back in his chair. He hadn't exactly expected her to fall into his arms and declare that she still liked him; that, in fact, she loved him after all of these years. But he had hoped there was still some emotion on her part—that she would be willing to give a relationship with him a chance. . .without him having to be a tutor while she worked to catch another guy's attention. He wasn't exactly planning a proposal—that would be too sudden. Maybe. Maybe not. They'd known one another forever, and over the course of the past few months, he'd grown closer to Maddy than he had to any other woman he'd dated. But in his heart, he knew. He'd been praying and struggling with his emotions for several weeks now. And he knew that given just the slightest encouragement from Maddy, he'd ask her to be his wife in an instant.

But it was too late for any of that. Maddy had been almost giddy with excitement as she'd told him about her own plans and her feelings for this man. And now, she felt sure of what to do. Not only was she going to finally tell the guy, but she wanted Jordan to listen to what she planned to tell the guy. When she'd asked for his help, Jordan had been too stunned to say anything but yes. It was his own fault, really. She told him that he himself had given her the idea. And he had. Only, he'd never really expected her to take him up on the offer. But she had. And upon his return on Monday night, he would have to sit down and listen to Maddy as she rehearsed with him how she would finally pour her heart out to another man.

After all of his prayers, he'd felt confident to have a heart-to-heart with Maddy and tell her he loved her. But she said she'd been praying too, and she thought it was time to tell this guy how she felt about him.

How could this be happening? Both he and Maddy had

based their decisions on their own prayers and what they felt the Lord had instructed.

Jordan frowned. Somehow, between he and Maddy, one of them was not hearing from the Lord correctly. And he had the sinking feeling that it might be him. Glancing at his watch, he realized if he didn't leave soon, he was going to be late for church.

I'm not going to give up unless You tell me to, Lord, he silently prayed as he left his hotel room.

≈

Sunday morning Maddy awoke bright and early. She'd spoken to Jordan the night before and he'd mentioned that he was still a little nervous about having to speak in front of the whole church. She called his hotel room, but there was no answer. She figured he must have left early.

But before she got ready to go to church, she got down on her knees and prayed.

"Lord, I just want to ask that You will wash Jordan with Your peace this morning, and take away any fear he has about sharing his story. I know it will be rough for him, so please hide him under the shadow of Your wings and let him feel Your protection. And I ask the same for myself for tomorrow. I know I need to have this conversation with Jordan, but I'm still a little jittery about it. Please give me the courage I need to make it through. And if Jordan doesn't feel the same about me, please help me not to feel too hurt about it, and don't let him feel any guilt. In Jesus' name, Amen."

When Maddy got up from her knees, she felt calm and unafraid. She smiled. "The truth has made me free," she told herself. "Well. . .almost."

≈

Maddy stared at the table one last time. The day had been ideal. Classes had gone well, and all the students and teachers had been in cheerful moods since it was the last week of the camp.

She'd been able to leave on time, and when she got home, she'd immediately set about preparing dinner for Jordan. First, she'd roasted a chicken with a rub of *herbs de Provence*, a mixture of basil, fennel seed, lavender, marjoram, rosemary, sage, summer savory, and thyme. Next, she oven roasted a spaghetti squash, which she knew was one of Jordan's favorites. She also prepared a simple Greek salad. For dessert, she'd made a raspberry sorbet the night before. The menu was simple, but she knew that Jordan really liked each of the dishes, because he'd said so when he'd taught her how to make them.

Now, she stood at the window, waiting for Jordan to arrive. It was ten after eight, and even though he was only a few minutes late, she was starting to worry that he might not come after all. Finally, she saw his SUV round the corner to her street. She ran back to the dining room and lit the candles on the table. Just as she was going back to the door, the phone rang.

Maddy sighed and hurried to pick up the extension in the living room. "Hello?"

"Maddy, it's me," her mother said. Her parents were having dinner at Mrs. Myston's house. "I just wanted to let you know that Jordan just pulled up."

Maddy laughed. "Yes, Mom. And I know you want to know what's happening, so I'll make it easy for you. I'll open the blinds in the dining room. That way, you can watch us eat dinner from Mrs. Myston's living room. Mrs. Myston won't even have to get out the binoculars."

Her mother laughed. "You don't think we would spy?" she asked in mock indignation.

"I didn't think you wouldn't," Maddy said. At that moment, the doorbell rang.

"I've got to answer the door, Mom. I'll get back to you later."

"Okay, sweetie. And Mrs. Myston told me to tell you that Jordan is all dressed up in a suit and tie, so it's a good thing you decided to wear your long turquoise dress. But I better let you go. Your dad says that if you don't open the door soon, Jordan's going to get suspicious."

"Then I'll go now." Maddy laughed.

She put down the receiver and went to the front door. Jordan stood on the steps, holding a single rose, surrounded by a variety of herbs. Holding them out to Maddy, he said, "I thought I'd bring these by for old times' sake. You can either cook the herbs or put them in a vase. The rose. . ." He tilted his head to the side. "I don't suggest cooking with the rose."

Maddy laughed and took the flowers and herbs. "Come on in," she said. Jordan stepped inside. Just before Maddy closed the front door, she caught a glimpse of her mother and Mrs. Myston in Mrs. Myston's living room window. Maddy shook her head and smiled to herself. If things didn't go well, she could count on them to be there for her in a matter of seconds.

Jordan was standing in the hallway, looking nervous.

"Why don't we eat dinner first?" she suggested. "That way you can tell me about yesterday."

Jordan nodded in agreement. "Let's get the easy part out of the way."

While they ate their dinner, Jordan told her what had happened.

"I was so nervous Saturday night that I got up early in the morning. I ended up leaving much earlier than I needed to, so I decided to walk around town. While I walked, I just prayed and prayed. After about an hour, I started to relax, and before I knew it I had made my way to the campus. While I walked, I thought about Malcolm, and I thanked God that Malcolm hadn't let me walk away from him that morning. I feel like it was truly God's hand on Malcolm that directed him to ask me that question. And I am so thankful that he didn't ignore me just because I'd already turned down the gospel so many times. And by the time I made it over to the church that morning, I wasn't nervous anymore. In fact, I couldn't wait for my turn to speak.

Maddy didn't interrupt, but waited for Jordan to finish.

"I had to wait for the entire sermon to end. Finally, right before the altar call, the pastor called me up to the podium. Malcolm's wife and her new husband introduced me, and I almost lost my courage while I stood there waiting for them to finish. But finally, it was my turn. I started out by telling everyone that I needed to make my public profession of faith. And then I just told them everything, pretty much the same way I told you. I started crying, and when I looked around, lots of other people were crying, too.

"By the time I finished my story, I felt totally bold. Before I even realized it, I started giving an altar call. And even though I had never, ever really witnessed to anyone, I started asking these people if they knew what their relationship with the Lord was. I told them that it was important to not waste any time when our eternity is at stake. I don't even know where I got the words from." He stared at Maddy and shook his head in disbelief. "The words just came to me. And before I knew it, people were coming to the altar and praying. And I'm no preacher. But I'm so glad that I was able to get up there and talk yesterday. Hopefully, somebody will remember my courage and be able to tell other people." He hung his head. "I'm just embarrassed that it took me so long to do it. But I'm glad I went. And I feel more encouraged to keep witnessing to my parents. Hopefully, one day, they'll actually listen to what I have to say instead of getting upset with me."

Maddy smiled. "I do, too. I'm so proud of you. And it looks like your testimony definitely had an impact on some people." She didn't say anything else, because she was starting to feel a little jittery about what she still had to do.

They spent the rest of the meal discussing different subjects, such as Maddy's job and Jordan's apartment. Finally, Jordan finished the last bite of his sorbet.

He looked down at his empty bowl and said, "Well, Maddy, the dinner was delicious. At least this guy will know you can cook." Then he asked, "Are you going to cook this same dinner for him, too?"

Maddy swallowed. It was time to start confessing. "Well. . . this dinner was planned for you since you like these dishes so much."

Jordan looked relieved. "I have to be honest with you, I didn't want you cooking my favorite dishes for some other guy."

Maddy was surprised. Was this an answer to her prayers? Was Jordan about to reveal that he had feelings for her? She paused, expectantly. Neither of them spoke for several moments.

Finally, Jordan said, "I guess it's your turn. Do you want to do this in here or the living room?"

"In here," Maddy said emphatically. "Is that okay with you?"

"Sure. I'll just sit here and play like I'm the guy. Go ahead and say what you need to say." He smiled, but looked uncomfortable.

Maddy swallowed. "I guess the best way to start is to just jump in. Please don't interrupt me. You can say whatever you want when I'm finished."

"Sounds fair to me," Jordan said stiffly.

Maddy cleared her throat and began. "It says in the Bible that the truth will set me free. And I'm telling you this because I need to be free. I started out trying to get your attention by learning how to cook. I thought that if I knew how to cook, it would make you take notice of me. But what I didn't realize was that I was only attracted to a small facet of you. And as I worked to impress that facet, I realized there was more of you I didn't really know. A good friend of mine kept telling me that a man should love me for who I am, not who I can make myself to be, but I didn't believe him." She paused and smiled at Jordan.

"The funny thing was, I found myself telling the same

thing to one of my students. And I got so frustrated with her when she didn't believe me. Ironically, she told me a few days ago that I was right. The only thing was, I realized that I wasn't practicing what I was preaching. I was telling her one thing and doing something totally different.

"So I've asked you here tonight so that I can be honest with you. A long time ago, I fell in love with my next-door neighbor. At least, I thought I was in love. But when I met him again, he wasn't the same person. I plotted and schemed about how I could get him to notice me, and I came up with the idea of getting him to teach me how to cook. But like I said, he wasn't the same person. And even though I thought I loved my next-door neighbor, I fell in love with my cooking teacher." Maddy stopped and drank a sip of water, while avoiding eye contact with Jordan.

"My cooking teacher is a great guy. He's a Christian. He's a very patient teacher who supported me, even though he thought I was making a mistake. And he became my friend, trusting me enough to share some very personal things with me. We pray for each other, we laugh and have fun together. When I realized I was falling in love with him, I started praying about it. I was scared to open up and be honest, but one day I was praying, and I remembered the verse that says the truth will set me free. I've been trying to hide it and deny it, but now I know for sure. And even though I don't know how he feels about me, I know I have to say this." Maddy took a deep breath and looked across the table, locking gazes with Jordan. "I love you, Jordan Sanders," she said simply. She held her hands to stop them from shaking.

Jordan opened his mouth, then closed it. Finally, he cleared his throat and said, "Are you sure?"

Maddy nodded, tears filling her eyes.

He exhaled loudly, then stood up and walked around to her side of the table. He pulled out the chair next to her and sat down. "Maddy, you don't know how happy I am that you told me this. I've spent this whole summer being jealous of your mystery crush. And it was me the whole time?"

"Yes," Maddy said, wiping her eyes. "How do you feel about that?"

He grinned. "I feel relieved. I've been praying and praying about how I feel. When you told me you were going to tell the guy, I felt like God hadn't heard any of my prayers. All day long I kept wondering how in the world I was going to react to your telling me that you were in love with some other guy." He took her hands and stood slowly, gently drawing her out of her chair.

The two stood for several moments, gazing into one another's eyes.

"So does this mean. . .?" Maddy trailed off, not quite knowing what to say.

"It means, Madison Thompson, I love you, too. Would you marry me?" said Jordan.

Maddy burst into tears mingled with laughter. "Of course. I was just getting nervous because it was taking you so long to ask."

He took her in his arms and kissed her. When he pulled away, Maddy grinned. "So did I graduate?" she asked.

"Graduate?" he repeated, confused.

"From wife school," she reminded him.

"Oh, yes, wife school," he said. His face grew serious and he was quiet for a few moments. Slowly, a smile spread across his face. "Yes, you've earned your wife degree. How about another kiss?"

Maddy put her hand in front of her face. "Not so fast, mister. What was my grade?"

"Hmm. . .I'd have to say A minus," he said as he leaned toward her.

"A *minus?*" she challenged. "Why not a solid A?"

Jordan lifted an eyebrow. "Surely you haven't forgotten those double-the-temperature-half-the-time chocolate chip cookies?"

"Oh," said Maddy. "I guess you're right. I'll have to settle for the A minus." She lifted her face to him and let him kiss her again.

When the kiss ended, Jordan said, "I think you just earned that A, Miss Thompson."

"That's more like it, Professor Sanders." She laughed.

A Letter To Our Readers

Dear Reader:

In order that we might better contribute to your reading enjoyment, we would appreciate your taking a few minutes to respond to the following questions. We welcome your comments and read each form and letter we receive. When completed, please return to the following:

Rebecca Germany, Fiction Editor
Heartsong Presents
PO Box 719
Uhrichsville, Ohio 44683

1. Did you enjoy reading *The Wife Degree?*
   ❑ Very much. I would like to see more books
      by this author!
   ❑ Moderately
      I would have enjoyed it more if _____

   _____

   _____

2. Are you a member of **Heartsong Presents**?   Yes ❑   No ❑
   If no, where did you purchase this book? _____

   _____

3. How would you rate, on a scale from 1 (poor) to 5 (superior), the cover design? _____

4. On a scale from 1 (poor) to 10 (superior), please rate the following elements.

   _____ Heroine   _____ Plot

   _____ Hero   _____ Inspirational theme

   _____ Setting   _____ Secondary characters

5. These characters were special because_____

_____

_____

6. How has this book inspired your life?_____

_____

_____

7. What settings would you like to see covered in future **Heartsong Presents** books?_____

_____

_____

8. What are some inspirational themes you would like to see treated in future books?_____

_____

_____

9. Would you be interested in reading other **Heartsong Presents** titles?   Yes ❏   No ❏

10. Please check your age range:
    ❏ Under 18   ❏ 18-24   ❏ 25-34
    ❏ 35-45   ❏ 46-55   ❏ Over 55

11. How many hours per week do you read?_____

Name _____

Occupation _____

Address _____

City _____ State _____ Zip _____

Grace Livingston Hill Collections

Readers of quality Christian fiction will love these new novel collections from Grace Livingston Hill, the leading lady of inspirational romance. Each collection features three titles from Grace Livingston Hill, and a bonus novel from Isabella Alden, Grace Livingston Hill's aunt and a widely-respected author herself.

Collection #8 includes the complete Grace Livingston Hill books *The Chance of a Lifetime*, *In the Way*, and *A Voice in the Wilderness*, plus *The Randolphs* by Isabella Alden.

paperback, 464 pages, 5 ¾₆" x 8"

❤ ❤ ❤ ❤ ❤ ❤ ❤ ❤ ❤ ❤ ❤ ❤ ❤

❤ ❤ ❤ ❤ ❤ ❤ ❤ ❤ ❤ ❤ ❤ ❤ ❤

·······Presents·······

Great Inspirational Romance at a Great Price!

Heartsong Presents books are inspirational romances in contemporary and historical settings, designed to give you an enjoyable, spirit-lifting reading experience. You can choose wonderfully written titles from some of today's best authors like Hannah Alexander, Irene B. Brand, Yvonne Lehman, Tracie Peterson, and many others.

When ordering quantities less than twelve, above titles are $2.95 each.
Not all titles may be available at time of order.

Heart♥ng Presents
Love Stories Are Rated G!

That's for godly, gratifying, and of course, great! If you love a thrilling love story, but don't appreciate the sordidness of some popular paperback romances, **Heartsong Presents** is for you. In fact, **Heartsong Presents** is the *only inspirational romance book club* featuring love stories where Christian faith is the primary ingredient in a marriage relationship.

Sign up today to receive your first set of four, never before published Christian romances. Send no money now; you will receive a bill with the first shipment. You may cancel at any time without obligation, and if you aren't completely satisfied with any selection, you may return the books for an immediate refund!

Imagine. . .four new romances every four weeks—two historical, two contemporary—with men and women like you who long to meet the one God has chosen as the love of their lives. . . all for the low price of $9.97 postpaid.

To join, simply complete the coupon below and mail to the address provided. **Heartsong Presents** romances are rated G for another reason: They'll arrive *Godspeed!*